About the Author

David McCaddon is an IT systems consultant who has worked in computing for over 46 years and has spent the past 34 years specialising in Law Enforcement Computer Systems Development. His investigative systems experience has seen him working with police forces worldwide in the design and development of major incident and analysis systems.

Dedication

This book is dedicated to my friends and family including those who ask whether any of the characters in my books and plays are based on anyone in particular. The answer is of course yes, some of you are in there somewhere!

David McCaddon

IN DIGITAL PURSUIT

AUSTIN MACAULEY PUBLISHERS™

LONDON • CAMBRIDGE • NEW YORK • SHARJAH

A CIP catalogue record for this title is available from the British Library.

ISBN 978-1-78710-121-0 (Paperback)
ISBN 978-1-78710-122-7 (E-Book)
www.austinmacauley.com

First Published (2017)
Austin Macauley Publishers Ltd™.
25 Canada Square
Canary Wharf
London
E14 5LQ

Acknowledgments

A huge thank you to Annabelle, Joan and friends for helping me with this novel, as ever your help and guidance is so very much appreciated.

PROLOGUE

Knutsford Crown Court – Monday 2nd November, 2015

'Timothy John Ridgway, you have been found guilty of forty-five counts of fraud – including thirty-seven counts of identity theft – and stealing funds amounting to several thousand pounds, some of which I am pleased to say has at least been recovered under the Proceeds of Crime Act 2002. I have now had time to consider all the facts and whilst the court takes into account that these are your first offences I can only conclude that you are a most devious criminal from whom the public needs protection and I have no hesitation in passing a sentence of ten years' imprisonment.

Take him down officer.'

CHAPTER 1

Tim Ridgway was handcuffed and still in a state of shock as the court's officer marched him down the narrow steps from the dock into a holding-room where all his possessions were taken from him, logged and sealed in a plastic bag. The officer removed the bag, exited and locked the room behind him. Whilst this lengthy process went on Ridgway couldn't help noticing a sign on the wall which stated *'Decency, Dignity and Respect. Help us deliver these things.'* He sat down alone in the room waiting to see what would happen next. He was still stunned by the outcome of the case.

It was a strange mixture of emotions he was now feeling, from relief that at last the long wait of getting his case heard was over, to one of anxiety on how he would cope in prison.

As he sat there he could hear the judge pronouncing sentence. Ten years, ten whole years, repeated over and over in his head.

After a short while the court officer returned and he was then moved into a cell where he was told to wait for the prison transfer van to arrive. Boredom had now set in so Tim decided to do press-ups just to pass the time. He knew he was unfit. After what seemed like hours, he was escorted down the long narrow corridor out of the court building into the secure yard and towards the waiting prison van. Somehow, even though he'd been held in custody for a period of three months and had had more than enough time to take it all in, he perhaps foolishly hadn't expected a custodial sentence. He had even made plans to go out that evening but they were now completely scuppered. He slowed his pace down as he approached the vehicle and suddenly felt his legs folding from underneath him as the prison officer opened up the rear door of the van.

'Come on! In you go, Ridgway. We can't mess about waiting for you. We have a long journey ahead of us and I want to get back for the United game,' and the burly prison escort bundled him up the step into the van.

'Where are you taking me?'

'Oh, you are lucky, mate! You are off to one of the new prisons – HMP Dinas Bay in North Wales.'

'I wouldn't exactly call it lucky.'

'Well, I bloody would! You haven't seen some of the others, mate. This will be like a luxury hotel compared to them! Come on – and get a move on. Get your arse in there! You are in cell one on the left hand side. Get in there, pronto.'

Tim Ridgway thought cell was too grand a word for it. So much for dignity and respect! He sat down on the moulded plastic seat in the small cubicle cell. He heard the door slamming locked behind him. This was another world, far from the lifestyle he had just started to get used to.

How had it all come to this, he thought. A promising computing career – and here he was, about to start a ten year prison sentence. The van stank of urine and disinfectant and Tim, who was now feeling claustrophobic, nearly choked with the stench and heaved with the smell. Clearly the vehicle had been cleaned out recently but years of prisoner transfers had ingrained the smell within it.

Suddenly, without any warning whatsoever, another prisoner in another cell started banging and kicking, effing and blinding and attempting to rock the vehicle.

'Get a move on, you bastards! Why are we bloody well waiting? Why are we waiting?'

The monotonous and tuneless singing of *'Why are we waiting'* continued, to the annoyance of Tim and everyone else in the van.

'Calm down, Redfern! Give it a rest or else you will have me to deal with,' came the reply from the prisoner escort officer.

'Oh yeah! Think you're big enough, pig? Come on in here and say that! You lot are all mouth and trousers. I shit you for breakfast,' came the reply.

'Oh, I'm big enough all right! You'll soon find out how big I am if I have to come in there! Now bloody well shut up! We'll be on the road soon.'

'Bastards! You're all just a bunch of bastards,' came the grunt of a reply.

Surprisingly then it went quiet and Tim, who had no idea who else was in the van, could now hear occasional weeping coming from an adjacent cell.

He then heard the rear doors slamming shut and he saw the driver and the other officer walking round to the cab. Minutes later he heard the engine starting and the van pulled away.

As the van left the court he looked out of the small smoked glass window. He could see out but no-one could see in. There was a flash of a camera and the usual small crowd of inquisitive passers-by and the odd photographer but certainly nowhere near the size of crowds you see typically on the TV news.

Within minutes they were heading out of the court complex and down the tree-lined road and across open parkland, heading towards the busy M6 motorway.

CHAPTER 2

DS Holdsworth was at his desk in Divisional HQ when he received the telephone call from his new boss, DI Chandler, who had recently transferred from the Drugs Squad.

'Jim, I want you and two selected members of your team to work on a special investigation that has just been placed on my desk. I know you are busy with card fraud investigations but DCI Bentley has just dropped this one on us as a matter of urgency and we have no choice in taking this on.'

'Right, sir. Can you tell me what this is all about? Do you have any more details?' enquired the DS, jotting the notes down in his diary.

'No, not at the moment, Jim – I'm afraid I can't. You know as much as I do. I also suggest that you choose the members of your team that you want with you once we have met and discussed the investigation. It could need some specialised skills so you will need to select carefully. Please attend a meeting tomorrow morning at the DCI's office in Force HQ at 8.30am sharp. It will be just you at this stage – but I'll be attending with you. Oh, and by the way, the chief will also be in attendance, so please be there in plenty of time. I'll see you in the morning and please not a word to anyone. Understood?'

'Understood! Will do, sir. I'll see you in the morning.'

DS Holdsworth replaced the receiver, wondering what it was that was so secretive about this particular investigation and what was so special that the Chief Constable himself was having to attend.

***

Whilst heading westbound across the busy M56, the prisoner transfer van received a radio call asking the escort officers to make a slight detour to collect an additional prisoner. Just forty-five minutes after leaving Knutsford the prison van pulled into Chester Crown Court alongside the river Dee. As the driver and his assistant got out of the van, the prisoner previously identified as Redfern started to kick off again and began thumping the sides of the van.

'What are we bleeding stopping for this time?' he shouted. 'Let me out! I'm bursting for a bloody piss.'

'Be quiet, Redfern. We'll be on our way as soon as we pick up another prisoner. This is not a bloody bus service you know! You'll just have to wait till we get there,' replied the driver.

'You're right there! It would make a shit bus service with you buggers in charge of it.'

'Calm down,' came the reply. 'We'll soon be on our way again.'

The rear doors opened and Tim could hear another prisoner being escorted into one of the remaining cells in the prison van and minutes later the doors were slammed shut and they were on their way again.

After a further two hour drive, which took them onto the very busy A55 dual carriageway and through several narrow lanes across the North Wales countryside, the prison van eventually arrived down the newly-laid tarmac driveway of HMP Dinas Bay. It was early afternoon and the rain was now lashing against the windows of the vehicle as it approached the imposing building. HMP Dinas Bay stood proud, perched on the cliffside almost castle like, overlooking the Irish Sea. The brand new Category C prison, which had only been open for just under twelve months, had been built on the site of what was originally an old disused stone quarry, and had wide far-reaching views across the sea to Anglesey and beyond. On a good day from here you could see the Irish coastline; on a bad day you couldn't even see your hand in front of you with infamous sea fog hugging the coastline. Before this prison had been opened, prisoners from the North and Mid Wales areas had to be housed in various prisons across the North West. It was not ideal for visitors but the prison service also had a clear need for additional prisons in the area, hence further plans to build an even bigger prison in North Wales at Wrexham.

Tim Ridgway watched through the van's window as the driver handed over his paperwork to the prison officer at the main gatehouse. After a short phone call from the gatehouse to the Control Room a large barrier was automatically lifted and the van moved forward about one hundred yards to a huge metal door which, on their approach, was electronically raised. The van entered the prisoner reception yard and came to a stop alongside a further, smaller security door. The huge metal door immediately closed behind the vehicle and Tim watched as one of the prisoner escort officers stepped down from the warmth of his cab and walked across into the secure prisoner reception area, leaving the driver to reverse the van right up to the security door.

'Ok, you lot – the mystery tour is over! Welcome to the seaside! Now, let's be having you,' cried the prison officer as he stepped up into the van. A group of prison officers were ready and waiting to process them. One at a time each of the four prisoners was led out to the two prisoner reception desks where they were each individually assessed and briefed to ensure they understood the prison rules and procedures. This was also the first time that Tim Ridgway had seen his fellow prisoners who had travelled in the van. A stocky, heavily tattooed man, who Tim assumed was the prisoner referred to as Redfern, (the one who had been doing all the shouting) was the first at the desk. He was now, with head bowed, somewhat subdued. Then followed a scruffy, long haired guy who was followed by a middle-aged, well-dressed grey-suited man who somehow seemed out of place.

Tim sat and watched while the two prisoners in front of him were checked in. After about ten minutes it was now the turn of Tim and the man in the grey suit to be processed as they walked up to their respective desks.

'Prynhawn Da, Croeso y Gymru and welcome to HMP Dinas Bay, Mr Ridgway,' said the prison officer in a strong Welsh accent. 'We just to need to go through the booking-in procedure which shouldn't take too long.'

Tim thought about saying he'd got all the time in the world but decided he would be better keeping quiet during this reception process.

He was now photographed having already been given his prison number. His property, which had been previously removed in the court, was now handed over to the prison officer.

'And where would you like your belongings sent to?' enquired the prison officer.

'I hadn't thought really – but if you could forward them to this address,' responded Tim, writing down Alan's details at the Jelly Bean café.

Tim was now escorted into a separate room, stripped and searched and given prison clothes: grey tracksuit bottoms and a prison polo shirt which fitted surprisingly well. Gone for the time being were his Givenchy and

Hugo Boss designer clothes which were now carefully bagged up and stored safely for his future release.

Tim thought the odd thing was that he had been allowed to keep his shoes which certainly looked out of place with his grey baggy tracksuit bottoms.

'I wouldn't worry too much about these. You can have your own jeans, tee shirts and trainers brought in soon,' advised the prison officer.

After completing what seemed an endless supply of paperwork, he was now the last prisoner to be processed and given his bundle of blankets, plastic cup and plate. He was then marched up a set of stairs through several locked doors which were signposted 'Medical Centre'. He finally arrived at his interim cell in the hospital wing.

'Why am I being placed in the medical centre? There is nothing wrong with me.'

'It's for your own safety, Mr. Ridgway. It's policy here that you spend your first twenty-four hours here as part of your induction process. The induction wing is full at present and that is why you will be here in the medical wing. It's an overflow and just a precaution in case you have any ideas about topping yourself. But why would you want to do that when you are surrounded by beautiful countryside with the Irish Sea on your doorstep! Now, don't get too comfortable in there. We'll be moving you into another cell in a day or two.'

Tim looked around the tiny cell in the medical wing as the door slammed shut behind him and thought no-one could be too comfortable in here. All he had was a narrow bed, a table and a stainless steel toilet and sink. He paced up and down. It was about 8 feet long and 5 feet wide. He looked through the bars of the tiny window but could see nothing apart from a twinkling light in the distance. It was now going dark and the night was setting in fast. The storm was brewing outside but at least he was warm in the cell. He could hear the wind howling and thought back to how in a short time he'd come from his luxurious executive penthouse apartment to this. He went over and lay on the bed, wrapped the blanket around him and rested his head on the rock-hard pillow. Soon tired and exhausted he dropped off to sleep but was awakened just a couple of hours later by a female prison officer.

'Tim, isn't it? Come on, wake up! Here is your evening meal,' she said politely, placing a small plate of burnt sausages and runny mash on the table in front of him. 'I'll be back later to collect everything.' The prison officer left immediately and re-locked the metal door.

Tim thought, room service and addressing me by my first name! I didn't expect that! It can't be bad. I bet it won't last. And he was right.

The food, however, looked disgusting – but Tim was very hungry. He was in a state of shock after the sentencing and had refused the sandwich offered to him in the court cell whilst waiting for the prison van. He wolfed down the lukewarm food and went back to his bed. He laid his head on the pillow and wept like he'd never wept before. After a few minutes he fell into a deep, deep sleep.

***

Tuesday 3rd November, 2015

'Ok Ridgway! Wakey, wakey! Time to get up! We can't have you being too comfortable in there,' came the shout through the small metal hatchway in the door. 'Come on – you're being moved today. It's 7.00 am. Now get dressed quickly as you can. You can have a shower in your new wing. I'll be back for you in ten minutes to take you to 'A' wing and you can have your breakfast down there.'

Tim was still tired. He'd been in a deep sleep for a couple of hours initially but then woke early and had not slept much after that. The bed was not the most comfortable he'd slept in and although the hospital wing had been quiet apart from the howling wind outside he'd had a restless night. He could still hear in his head the sentence being read out loud by the judge. He noticed that his evening meal, plate and tray had mysteriously disappeared, presumably when he was in a deep sleep. He slowly wrenched himself off the bed and looked out of the tiny barred window. Dawn was just breaking. For a prison it offered a great view overlooking the rocks and the crashing waves of the Irish Sea way down below. In the distance he could just make out what looked like a small fishing boat on the horizon. He brushed his teeth and splashed cold water over his face,

21

slipped back into the tracksuit bottoms and tee shirt and sat back down on the bed to wait for the prison officer. He didn't have to wait long as the door was unlocked and a tall, thick-set, heavily-built officer with a clipboard stepped in.

'This way, Ridgway. Bring your blanket and everything with you. Here's a plastic bag you can put them in. I'm here to escort you to your new home in 'A' wing.'

Tim collected together his so-called hygiene pack, blanket, plastic plate and mug that had been previously issued to him on arrival. He placed them all in the large plastic bag as advised and they stepped into the corridor. They made their way through a maze of locked metal doors and gates, the prison officer unlocking and re-locking the doors as they made their way down a labyrinth of corridors through to a central area with wide landings going off at different angles. The glass-screened control room housed a number of prison officers who could keep a watchful eye on each of the spurs. They headed down the corridor through several locked gates marked 'A' wing and finally arrived at their destination and checked in with the duty wing prison officer.

'Welcome to Block 'A'. You're just in time for breakfast, Ridgway, but first let's find your cell. Ah yes! Let me see, you are in A112. Down here! You can drop your stuff off there in your cell and then I suggest you get some breakfast before it's all gone.'

Tim was then escorted down the wing and onto a landing which housed a row of cells. The metal doors were now open and he could see they were all two-bedded cells and could smell the smoke from prisoners probably having their first cigarette of the day. He was wondering what his fellow cell inmate would be like – hopefully not a smoker, he thought, as he couldn't stand the smell. He would complain if so, although deep down he knew he didn't really have any choice whatsoever in the matter. He remembered reading that eventually all prisons would be smoke-free as it is in other countries. But for now this was 2015 and he had to make the best of it.

'You are in here, on the right. Enjoy your stay with us! I am sure we will all get along just fine as long as we behave,' remarked the prison officer, who then left him to get on with meeting his new cellmate. Tim entered the cell apprehensively and that was when he received his first surprise of the day.

***

DS Holdsworth had decided to have an early night if he was to be up early for the meeting at Force HQ. Since his divorce three years ago he'd lived on his own in a rented flat in Cheadle about ten miles from Divisional HQ. He badly missed his two children whom he only saw at weekends but he had soon become quite settled with his new bachelor lifestyle existence. He was dedicated to his job as a police officer. It had been his desire to serve in the police service ever since leaving school. Jim, however, was a workaholic and this in itself had primarily led to the breakdown of his marriage. Since entering CID he had worked endless unsociable hours, dropped out of no end of family events, missed seeing his children growing up, had constant rows with his wife and inevitably something had to give. He had set the alarm for six but he didn't need it – he had been awake since the early hours, pondering on what it was that was so important that the Chief Constable himself needed to attend the meeting.

After a quick shower and a hasty breakfast and just slightly ahead of the rush hour he drove his grey Volvo estate down the A34 dual-carriageway and through the wet Manchester streets. He parked in the Force HQ car park, took the stairs to the third floor and signed in at the CID reception desk. He could see that DI Chandler was already sitting at the table in the DCI's office.

'Good morning, sir. Good morning, sir,' said DS Holdsworth, nodding across to the DCI as he knocked on the open door and entered the office.

'Good afternoon, DS Holdsworth. I'm glad you could make it. We were just talking about you. The chief should be with us any time,' smiled DCI Bentley – joking but with an element of sarcasm.

DS Holdsworth considered replying but thought better of it as he looked at his watch; it had just turned 8am. The DCI was not a bad old sort but he did have a way of winding people up the wrong way. Just then – and almost on cue – the Chief Constable, John Adams, arrived and closed the office door behind him. John Adams was one of the new breed of chief constables. He'd progressed rapidly through the ranks and been recognised from his early days in the force to be worthy of the top corridor. He had the utmost respect from his fellow officers - particularly those in CID, where he had served for many years. The officers in the room immediately stood to attention and exchanged good mornings before taking their seats at the small conference table.

'Well, we may as well start. I think everyone is here,' announced the Chief as he took a seat at the end of the table and opened his leather-bound folder. 'Now, what I'm about to tell you can go no further, apart from those officers who are going to be assigned to the case that I'm about to outline. For some time now we have been alerted to suspicions that an organised crime gang is operating in one of our prisons and that they are planning something on a very large scale, and I mean a very large scale. We don't know exactly what at this stage, as our informant who, incidentally, has only just been released from prison himself, couldn't tell us much more. We believe it may involve some form of large financial fraud but again that's supposition on our part.'

'Which prison are we talking about sir?' enquired DI Chandler, who was busy scribbling down notes.

'Ah, that we do know! It's one of the new ones – HMP Dinas Bay on the North Wales coast. We believe

25

that this gang consists of a core of key individuals supported by a few clusters of external so-called specialists and with a large network of close associates.'

'With great respect, Dinas Bay is off our patch, sir. Shouldn't the Gwynedd Valley Police be investigating this one in the first instance?' asked DCI Bentley, trying to be as diplomatic as possible.

'Well, they are involved, of course. We have been in touch with their local intelligence section but our informant has told us that he believes the ringleaders are all from our area. We have therefore agreed that we should be allocated the initial investigation.'

'Can we get a list of the prisoners who are from this area, sir? At least we may be able to whittle it down a bit and try to get a clearer understanding of who and what we might be dealing with here,' asked DS Holdsworth.

'Yes, we are on to that, detective sergeant. The prison establishment at HMP Dinas Bay I believe holds some 750 prisoners of which we understand over forty are from our area. It may be of course that our informant is mistaken and not all the gang are actually from around here. Nevertheless we'll get the list to you as a starting point.'

'Presumably the NCA (National Crime Agency) have also been informed sir?' asked DS Holdsworth, somewhat confused.

'Yes, the NCA have also been informed but at this stage they have agreed they will leave it to us to perform initial investigations only and then get involved as and when they are needed. Now, clearly we don't want to go in there heavy-handed just yet and alert the gang. In fact we don't even want the prison to know. We need to find out much more about what exactly is going on, on the inside; what they are planning, times, dates and so on, and that is where you come in, DS Holdsworth. We want you to be the team leader reporting to DCI Bentley and as we need to carry out covert surveillance on the gang, we are asking for a member of your team to go undercover.'

'Surely you are not suggesting we send in one of our officers, sir?' said DCI Bentley uncomfortably.

'That's exactly what I'm suggesting DCI. We need to send in someone to HMP Dinas Bay as soon as possible.'

CHAPTER 3

Tim (or prison number DB0267 as he was now known) entered the cell, where, to his complete surprise, waiting for him sitting reading on the bed was Charlie Ellis, his ex-partner in crime.

'Good God Charlie, I didn't expect to see you here! And if I did, I certainly didn't think we would be sharing a cell together. I heard you were in a Liverpool prison. I'm gob-smacked! This is a pleasant surprise! I'd have thought the powers-that-be would have separated us.'

'Hi, Tim, please keep your voice down,' whispered Charlie, getting up to shake Tim's hand. 'Welcome to Dinas Bay! Yes, I thought it might be you when they told me this morning that a new inmate called Ridgway was coming and would be sharing the cell with me. The chap who was in here before was transferred to another prison first thing this morning. I bet they haven't even made the connection between us. They are probably too busy to bother researching prisoner backgrounds. I think they are overstretched cell-wise so this of course might only be a temporary measure. They are probably likely to move you into another cell, possibly in another wing. Still, it's good to see you after all this time. You look well, apart from your attire that is. I must say it's a bit of a come-down from the clothes I last saw you in. Tell me – what sort of stretch did you eventually get?'

'I see you are already speaking the lingo, Charlie! I got ten years – and I'm thinking I will appeal. I don't know how I'm going to cope to be quite honest; my mind is a whole mix of emotions. Naturally I'm pleased that the court case is finally over but nervous and anxious about what exactly lies ahead here, I still have to wait for the outcome of the Jackson case as well. I really need to rethink my life. I've been stupid, really bloody stupid,' replied Tim as he sat on the vacant bed.

'Oh, you'll cope somehow. I've only been here a couple of weeks. They transferred me from HMP Bromsgrove. It's not a bad place here. Everything is relatively new and you will soon get into a daily routine. As you can see we've got a telly in each cell. If you want my opinion it's best not to dwell on the outside world – just forget all about it and move on. You'll be allocated a job here soon and although the pay is crap, at least it will keep you busy and help you to take your mind off things. Just keep your head down and keep out of any trouble is the best advice I can give you. There are a few people you need to be aware of though. Most of the prison officers are fine but there's the odd one who might give you grief – such as Henderson. I'd give him a wide berth if you can. You'll also soon find out the inmates you need to steer clear of on the wing.'

'So, what sort of job have you ended up with?'

'I've ended up in the kitchen! Imagine me, of all people, in the kitchen! I couldn't even make a piece of toast before. As it happens, I'm not due in there until after breakfast today.'

He got up and walked over to stare through the barred window.

'So what's the food like here, Charlie? Not up to much I suppose?'

'Oh, you'd be surprised – the food is not bad at all. Of course I'm biased but it's probably on a par with what you would have had in the Midshire Police canteen, I would have thought.'

'I bloody hope not! I always took my own butties in there. I'll starve to death first!'

Tim continued to stare out of the cell window across the grey, choppy sea. 'I tell you what though, I didn't expect a sea view! It's not bad at all.'

'Yes, I think most of this wing has that advantage. I think the neighbouring 'B' wing faces the rock face of the old quarry. Anyway, come on – let's go and get some breakfast before it all goes! Don't forget your plate, mug and plastic cutlery – and you'll have to wash them yourself afterwards. You can bring your breakfast back to the cell if you want to but you'll spend enough time in here as it is.'

They made their way across the landing and into the canteen area. Each wing had its own dining-hall which was serviced by a centralised kitchen area. This was the first real opportunity for Tim to see some of his fellow inmates on 'A' wing. He was unshaven and badly in need of a shower. As they took their place in the queue an inmate spotted the new man on the block. Tim started to feel uncomfortable, he could now feel a number of them eyeing him up. After collecting a breakfast of tea, toast with bacon and beans they took their seats in the corner. They had only been sitting down for about a minute when another inmate came over and sat across from Tim Ridgway.

'New boy, eh, new to this wing at least. So, what's your name then, new boy?' asked the inmate in a menacing manner.

'Ridgway,' responded Tim, trying to get on with his breakfast.

'Posh boy eh? Just arrived, I fancy. I've not seen you before. Well, I'm Higson and I run the joint around here! I'm the daddy – ok? – so don't bleeding forget it! Did you bring in a package?'

'A what?'

'A package, something we can help you retrieve,' replied Higson, who was clearly getting impatient.

'I haven't a clue what on earth you are on about,' said Tim through a mouthful of beans.

'Have you got any burn?' asked Higson, leaning over into Tim's personal space.

The inmate was so close Tim could smell his foul breath.

'Any what?' said Tim, clearly puzzled.

'Burn! Don't you know anything! Tabs, burn, snout, tobacco! Or does a fag mean different things to you, sunshine?'

'I don't smoke,' replied Tim, trying desperately to get on with his breakfast.

'Well, Posh Boy, now is a good time to start! Perhaps I can help you get started, then maybe move you on to something a bit stronger,' snarled Higson, leaning into Tim.

Tim continued to ignore him and carried on with his breakfast.

Just then a prison officer, who had been observing the conversation from a doorway, came over.

'Do we have a little problem here, gents?'

'No, no problem here officer, just having a nice conversation over breakfast,' said Charlie, coming to the rescue. 'Higson here was just welcoming Tim to our wing and he was about to return to his own table.'

'Good, well let's keep it that way. I think you were eating over there, Higson,' said the prison officer, pointing to another table. 'Perhaps you should return to finish your breakfast? Or of course we can always do with another pair of hands washing up in the kitchen!'

At this point Higson mumbled something inaudible, glared at Tim and slunk off to his own table, allowing Tim to continue his breakfast in peace.

'Don't let that bother you, Tim. I should have warned you about Higson but there are worse than him around this place,' said Charlie. 'Come on, finish that! You said you needed the shower block.'

***

Wednesday 4th November, 2015

DC Jack Hodgson was enjoying a couple of weeks off at home. He always took time off in the autumn just to recharge his batteries and complete the huge list of chores his wife had prepared for him. He thought it was wonderful to have a lie-in in the morning, ignore shaving and work only when he wanted to. But he'd kept himself busy. The kids were still in school and the whole place had needed a good sort-out. He'd lost count of the number of trips to the council tip he'd made in the last few days but he felt good, he'd earned lots of brownie points and the whole house and garden had been subjected to a very early spring clean – or a late one – depending on how you looked at it. It had been so mild weather-wise he'd even managed to mow the lawns. He had just finished preparing the bonfire for the fireworks party they were having later in the week and was clearing the last of the leaves off the front lawn into the wheelie bin when he got the call on his mobile from DS Holdsworth.

'Good morning, Jack. DS Holdsworth here. I'm really sorry to trouble you when you are on leave.'

'Actually, sarge, I'm on leaves!'

'What?'

'Nothing, sarge – just my little joke.'

'Right. Now look, Jack – as I say, I really am sorry to trouble you but is there any possible chance you can come into the office this afternoon? Say at two o'clock. I wouldn't ask but a bit of an urgent job has cropped up?'

'Yes, no problem, sarge! Be glad to get out of some of the remaining chores on my list! Gives me a good excuse!'

'Great. Can you please apologise to Sue? I'll see you in my office at 2pm.'

Jack Hodgson replaced the receiver, glanced at his watch and wondered what it was that could be so urgent. He was due back in the office on Monday anyway! Why wouldn't it wait until then? He decided he'd better clean himself up ready for the meeting so he discarded his gardening clothes and headed straight to the bathroom for a quick wash and change.

CHAPTER 4

DC Hodgson arrived – unshaven – at Divisional HQ just before 2pm for his meeting with DS Holdsworth. He hadn't dared to tell his wife that he was going into work. And if he'd had a shave she might have got suspicious. He was in enough trouble with Sue working the hours he did. He had lost count of the number of times he'd missed dinner through working unplanned overtime. As he walked into the office he was greeted by Ted Wilson, the civilian indexer in their squad.

'Good afternoon, Jack. I thought you were on leave. Can't you keep away from the bloody place?'

'Hi, Ted! I've been summoned to see the DS urgently. Not certain what the score is here. I'm due back anyway next week, so it beats me what the urgency is! Still, it's better than working at home.'

He picked up his post from the filing trays.

'Sounds like you might need a book down the back of your trousers Jack! Oh, and by the way, you've got something on your face! Let me know how you get on,' said Ted, pointing to Jack's chin and laughing out loud.

'Yes, thank you, smart arse! I'll let you know,' replied Jack as he entered the DS's office.

'Afternoon, Jack. Come on in,' said DS Holdsworth. 'Good to see you again! Come in and please shut the door behind you. Nice beard: it suits you!'

'Good afternoon, sarge. Yes, thank you, but not sure if I'm keeping it yet. I was just wondering what's so urgent that you needed me in so quickly? Oh, and by the way, if you see my missus, I haven't been here! All right? She thinks I'm down the pub.'

'No problem there, Jack. What I'm about to tell you must not go any further, right?'

'You know you can trust me, sarge.'

'Yes, I realise that and that's why I've asked you in. You are definitely the man for the job – particularly with your background working undercover. And come to think of it, the beard might come in handy.'

'Oh God, it's been a while since I've been undercover.'

'Yes, I appreciate that – but this job's a little bit special. The chief constable himself is overseeing it.' And he went on to brief DC Hodgson as to the meeting he had had the previous day with the Chief Constable and the DCI.

'So what role exactly do you see me playing in this, sarge?'

'Well... How do you fancy living in North Wales for a short time?'

'Bloody hell, you are joking, aren't you sarge? How long is a short time? My missus will kill me. I've only just got into credit with brownie points this week catching up on chores. '

'No, I'm not joking, and I can't say how long for definite, but the plan is this: we need you to go undercover again, this time at HMP Dinas Bay.'

'Undercover! As I say, I haven't done that for years. But I'm up for it if needed. HMP Dinas Bay? Isn't that the new privately-run prison that opened recently? Eh, hang on just a minute! This is not as a prisoner, I hope?'

'No, that had crossed our mind, but we'll save you from that! It probably wouldn't work – and we wouldn't wish that on you. Yes, it's one of the latest prisons. We've made arrangements with HMP HQ in London for you to work in the prison as a transferred prison officer. The HMP HQ intel section know a little about this as clearly we have had to take them at least into confidence, but, they don't have the full story. The prison itself doesn't have a clue and that's how we want to keep it.

'They think you have transferred from a prison down in the south west. Don't worry, you'll get the basic training you'll need beforehand. You will join the security team there and have access to the Intelligence Reports. That way we can get a good feel for what is actually going on in there. No one in the prison knows your real identity, not even the governors. As far as they are concerned you are an experienced prison officer and have transferred to fill a vacancy in their busy security department.'

'So, when do I start, sarge?'

'Like I say, I've arranged for you to have some basic training. Well, to be quite honest, it's no more than a day's briefing actually, from a recent HMP security officer. His name is John Hughes and he is currently on leave and originally from this area. He is about to retire. He spent a long time in security at HMP Exeter House and is coming here on Monday to spend a day with you, briefing you on the prison service, the security role itself, any background, and so on. That way no-one will suspect anything. He doesn't know why he is training you exactly but he thinks you are investigating possible prison officer corruption in a prison in the south east. He is someone we believe we can trust and is a personal friend of the DCI. If you go for training to any of the HMP establishments they may get wise and someone might blab something on the grapevine. We have arranged for your prison uniform to be sent to us so that you are equipped when you get there. You will be issued with the correct prison epaulettes on your arrival. This is standard practice with HMP transfers. Just let me know your chest, waist, height, and shoe sizes. Email me when you get back home today and we can get you fully kitted out.'

'But when do you want me to start, boss?'

'Ah, yes! Sorry about this, but this is the bad news! We do need you to get started as soon as possible – at the prison, on Monday 16th November at 8am sharp.'

'Bloody hell! So which prison is it that I am supposed to have transferred from?'

'Actually, this is the story. You have been on secondment recently to HMP HQ in London for the past two years working on research on whether biometric access would work within prison areas. Before that you spent over fifteen years in HMP Exeter House, if anyone asks. I suggest you swot up on biometric access, just in case anyone asks you anything about it. As it happens, it is something our own IT department has been looking at, so they will have plenty of background reading material on it. I suggest you call the Head of IT for some bedtime reading.'

'And will it work?'

'Will what work?'

'Biometric access in prison areas!'

'Oh! Right! Search me! I haven't a clue! Look, I suggest you read up on that just in case you get asked. You never know, one or two of the governors in HMP Dinas Bay may seek your opinion on it.'

'Right, sarge. And where am I supposed to stay in North Wales? It's way too far to do a daily commute from here and as a prison officer I wouldn't think my salary would run to a nice hotel for that length of time?'

'Right, we've thought of that! This is the story, OK Jack? You are waiting to sell your house back in Devon to move to the area, so for the time being you are staying alone in a static caravan that you are renting on the Lleyn Peninsular about ten miles south of Caernarvon. Your family from Devon will join you when you move into your new house. We have already booked and paid for the caravan for a three month stay. Hopefully you'll be well gone before then. Now from the caravan site, it's a short drive to the prison and the site is open all year round. I'm sure you will be fine there. This time of year it is likely to be quiet – you might even find you have the entire place to yourself. We will give you everything you need when you come in next week. I suggest you travel up there a week on Sunday to settle in.'

'Do we have an operation name for this, sarge?'

'Yes, it will be officially known as Operation Griffin.'

'Aren't griffins renowned for guarding treasure and priceless possessions?'

'Yes, but in this case you're guarding priceless intelligence!'

'Right. So how do I keep in touch with you guys? Presumably it's on the mobile after hours?'

'You don't as such. Well, that's not strictly true. Clearly we will expect a weekly report from you and we will keep in touch with you. Remember you cannot take mobile phones into the prison and we wouldn't want you to, anyway. You will, however, get access to a specific cloud portal. This is highly secure and you can log in from the new laptop we will provide you with and which will have to remain hidden in the caravan under lock and key when you are at work. Access will be a combination of fingerprint, retina and encrypted password. The portal will enable only you to leave encrypted messages, reports and so on and receive notifications/questions from us. You will get an hour's training on this when you come in next week. The IT guys know it is allocated to our department but clearly they have no knowledge of where you will be using it.'

'Well, that's straightforward enough. But what name do I go under?'

'That's easy! You're taking on the name of John Hughes, the guy who is actually training you, so you will have the right background should anyone check. You'll receive a briefing pack next week on everything you need to know about him. He doesn't know that you are taking his identity, temporarily of course.'

'Sounds like I've got some background reading to do, sarge.'

'You certainly have, Jack. Well, that's about it for now. Oh and keep the beard just in case anyone does happen to recognise you from the past. It's unlikely that you will have to work in the wings as such. I'll see you on Monday. Oh, and just one more thing, please pass on my best wishes to your wife and of course say nothing about this to anyone. Just tell Sue you are going on, say, a CID course, should she ask.'

'Oh, she'll bloody ask, all right! Guaranteed she'll ask!'

***

He changed into his shorts, tee shirt and trainers and made his way down the corridor to the Fitness Centre. The air-conditioned, well-equipped gymnasium, which was situated just off wings 'A' and 'B,' was always quieter just after meal times.

It was lunch time and always the ideal time to come and discuss the progress and review of their plans without being overheard. It was quieter than normal and, as he took his position on the cross trainer, he set the parameters for a casual 30 minute workout.

Soon he was joined by his collaborator.

CHAPTER 5

'You are doing what?' shouted a very red-faced Sue Hodgson, who was about to throw the dinner plate at him. Sue had quite a temper and could blow up at a minute's notice. Jack always said she could start a row in an empty house. Almost from the first day they were married they had endured a fiery relationship, but in the main they got on well together, despite both having busy lives and bringing up two delightful children.

'I'm going on a CID course, love. Look, it's been a while since I've attended a CID training course and – you never know – it might lead to a promotion, a bit more money each month coming in. It was too good an opportunity to turn down and I've already said yes to Jim Holdsworth now.'

Jack Hodgson had clearly raised the subject at the most inappropriate time and hated lying to his wife. He was now trying desperately to calm the situation down.

'And when are you going?'

'Next Sunday the 15th, love. It's short notice, I know, but it's not Jim Holdsworth's fault. He had only just heard about it himself.'

'Next Sunday! I'm sick of hearing about Jim sodding Holdsworth! So, how long is this bloody course exactly?'

'I'm not quite sure Sue, but I'll keep in touch. I may be able to get back home occasionally. Come on, love – you know our relationship always grows stronger after I've been away for a few weeks. Remember when we got together again after the last time I went away? Remember that weekend in Paris? I mean how could you forget that?'

'That was a long time ago! You won't get around me this time! But this seems bloody indefinite. I mean – will you be home for Christmas?'

'Yes, of course I will! Well, hopefully!' replied Jack, as the plate hit the wall behind him.

***

Tim Ridgway had cut himself shaving on the cheap disposable razor and prison soap he'd been given in his hygiene pack. He came out of the shower totally refreshed and dried himself off as best he could using the small prison towel he'd been given. He quickly got changed back into his tracksuit bottoms and tee shirt and made his way back down the corridor to the empty cell.

Charlie was still at work in the canteen. He sat down on the bunk bed and thought back to the lifestyle he'd recently started to enjoy in his luxury penthouse in Manchester. Even his girlfriends had abandoned him as soon as he was arrested. He was still going through the despair of it all, going from what had been a steady career in IT, a safe job which, although he found it boring at times, at least paid his bills. How could he have been so foolish? He must have known he'd have got caught searching PNC in the first place. He knew very well it was audited, but his burning desire to try and find the driver that had killed his parents all those years ago had driven him on. Then after his dismissal from the force the greed had set in as he slipped down the funnel of cyber-crime. He knew if he was to get through his years in prison he just had to pull himself together somehow and not dwell on this.

His thoughts were interrupted when Charlie walked in, back from his chores in the prison kitchen.

'Cheer up Tim! Come on, it's time for the exercise yard any time now. Come on – the fresh sea air will do you good.'

'It'll take more than fresh sea air to do me any good.'

They both made their way down the corridor and joined the queue out on to the exercise yard. The rain had stopped and if it wasn't for the high grey wall and razor wire it was almost pleasant in the weak autumn sunshine. Tim and Charlie wandered aimlessly around the perimeter of the yard watched over by several prison officers at various points. Although they couldn't see the sea from inside the yard they could hear the waves crashing onto the rocks and the subsequent rippling on the pebbled beach below. Tim could now see Higson in the far corner, preoccupied in a huddle talking to three other prisoners. They were far too busy talking to take any notice of Tim.

'Best to ignore them, Tim. Avoid any eye contact, for God's sake,' said Charlie. 'Just don't look at them or you'll find them coming after you.'

'They don't bother me,' shrugged Tim, kidding himself.

They continued walking and chatting about how they had ended up in prison, how they were eventually caught by the police and their treatment in custody.

'I bet you miss your old IT job back at Midshire Police, Tim?'

'No, not really Charlie. Why do you ask?'

'Well, I guess, like me, you must go over what might have been.'

'No, I believe in fate, Charlie. I think your life is mapped out for you. We all make mistakes and take the wrong turning now and again. However I certainly miss some of the people I used to work with. They were not a bad bunch when I think back to it. Apart from Paul Arrowsmith. He was a right clever bastard. We never got on. I was convinced he'd had it in for me all along, and I think it was him who shopped me to the Professional

Standards Department. In hindsight I wished I'd planted that porn stuff on his laptop just to wipe the grin off his bleeding face.' Tim had lost count of the circuits they had walked when the hooter blasted for their return to their wing. The prisoners formed an orderly queue and reluctantly filed back inside the prison block.

***

Thursday 5th November, 2015

Jean Price, one of the top Midshire Police crime analysts, was just popping out for lunch when she was called into DS Holdsworth's office.

'Jean, I'm really sorry to hold you up from your lunch, but please come in and close the door.'

'Yes, sergeant. Is there a problem, how can I be of help?'

'No, there is nothing the matter, Jean. Quite the contrary. Please come in and take a seat. I have a new assignment which I need to discuss with you rather urgently.'

'Jean, where shall I start? We've been impressed with your work, particularly the investigative analysis you did on the card fraud and vehicle theft incidents and I know you work well with DC Hodgson. A job has come up which is a little bit out of the ordinary, well, it's very much out of the ordinary, to be frank. I think you would be ideal to take on the role we need. It's a hush hush job and you must not discuss it with anyone. Understood?'

'Understood. I'm all ears, sergeant. Tell me more.'

'Well, the operation will be known as Operation Griffin. This is highly confidential, so you really must not discuss this with anyone other than the DCI, myself or DC Hodgson.'

The DS was firmly making the point and then continued to brief her on the planned surveillance activity and outlined what they knew so far.

'So, what exactly do you see as my role in this?' she asked.

'As I say, it's somewhat different to your role as a crime analyst but nevertheless it still requires some of those skills. I want you to be the liaison officer to DC Hodgson, who will be undercover. You will be his primary contact and your codename will be Eagle. Also of course we need you to deal with any intelligence we get from him and manage the case on the XIM investigative database. As of Monday 16th November, you will know him as John, John Hughes, who is an HMP officer. His codename is Lion. You will contact him on a dedicated mobile number only at specified times when we need to speak with him but most of the time it will be via his reports and online teleconference meetings. He will liaise with you via a secure encrypted message system from his laptop. I suggest for the time being that we start a new private case in XIM. We can move it to a HOLMES incident if need be, should it become a force-wide investigation later on. This data must not be subjected to the triggering/data comparison in the normal way. Essentially we want to know if there are any connections in any other case data, crimes, incidents and so on that we should know about. However, we don't want our data to alert other users. There should be only me and you with access to that data, no one else.

That will be all for now, Jean, I suggest whilst on this operation you take the spare desk in my office. Go off and get your lunch – and let's get started this afternoon.'

CHAPTER 6

Monday 9th November, 2015

DC Hodgson arrived in the office early on the Monday morning. To be honest he was glad to come to work having suffered a wall of silence all weekend. The fireworks party on the Saturday hadn't gone down too well because of the wet weather. The rain held off for about thirty minutes while Jack took charge of the fireworks display but Sue had not taken the news lightly that he was about to go away for several weeks. She suspected that in this new job there was more than meets the eye – but after years of living with him she would never press him for more information.

When he arrived at his desk there was a huge parcel waiting for him. He opened one end and he could see it was the prison security uniform that DS Holdsworth had ordered. He stored it in his locker and he was just starting to wade through two weeks of emails and messages when he got the call from reception saying that his visitor had arrived. He cleared his desk and made his way downstairs to reception to meet his trainer for the day. On arrival he could see John Hughes through the glass partition, sitting reading the internal force newsletter in reception. John was of similar build but slightly older than Jack Hodgson and somewhat ironically he also sported a beard.

'Good morning! You must be John Hughes,' said DC Hodgson, offering his hand. 'I'm Detective Constable Jack Hodgson. I'm pleased to meet you and thank you for coming over.'

'No problem, Jack. Glad I can be of any help. And just to reassure you, I will be saying nothing about our meeting.'

And he tapped the side of his nose.

'You certainly can help, John. We have the small conference room booked for just the two of us and I have a stack of questions I need to ask you.'

They made their way down the corridor into the small conference room.

'I'll organise us some coffee in a minute but please sit yourself down, and first of all tell me a bit about yourself,' said Jack, using the opportunity to gather as much as he possibly could about the background of his visitor.

John Hughes sat down and immediately went into great detail on not only his entire career but also moved on to his hobbies, pets and even his past, present and future holidays in fine detail – and almost to the point of boredom. Jack made notes and was beginning to regret he'd even asked but he needed the main points covered just in case anyone became suspicious of him at HMP Dinas Bay.

'Well, tell me about your security role in HMP Exeter House,' said Jack, trying to get him off his in-depth discussion on the history of canal boats and back onto the subject that he really needed to know more about.

After several hours and numerous coffees later DC Hodgson had found out all that he needed to know with regard to the processes in HMP security departments – although in a previous role as force liaison officer with the Manchester prison he had already gained a reasonable knowledge of the role that he was about to take on. He then showed John Hughes to the door – tired, exhausted and hoarse after the experience.

***

Tim Ridgway had now been in prison for seven days and was starting to get somewhat settled there in his cell with his old mate, Charlie. He'd now been allocated his job within the prison and was assigned to the Laundry. He'd hoped he could have joined Charlie in the kitchen but this was not to be as there was a queue a mile long for that type of job. The kitchen was seen as a much sought-after work role which enabled inmates to spend many more hours out of their cell and of course had the distinct benefit of access to more food. Tim, however, was satisfied for the time being with his role, despite the wages of just £7 per week which he put towards phone credits and canteen snacks. He'd been told by one of the prison officers in charge that, if he stuck at it and kept his nose clean, he could gain a Guild of Laundry & Dry-Cleaning Certificate and NVQ level 2. He had no intention whatsoever to do any such thing as Tim was already now planning his escape.

Tim had just completed his work for the day and returned to his cell exhausted at 4pm when the bell rang for 'Association'. For those prisoners who are not in education or working in the prison, this is the only real time an inmate gets to be let out of his cell for any length of time. This is a time when they can get together and a number of them opt to watch the television or play pool, table tennis, cards or dominoes.

Tim decided he now needed to make a phone call to Alan at the Jelly Bean Café. He had been given his pin number to make telephone calls from the Pin Phone on the wing. As usual there was a long queue but Tim decided to sit it out. Eventually it was his turn and, having previously notified the on-duty prison officer of the numbers he planned to dial, he rang the Jelly Bean café. He got through straight away and could sense by the noise that the place was as busy as ever.

'Alan, it's Tim! How are you?' he shouted amongst the din.

'Good to hear from you, Tim. I'm fine but, more important, how are you? I was so sorry to hear about the sentence. Are they treating you well?'

'Yes, I'm fine. Look, I'm at HMP Dinas Bay in North Wales. Can you please come over for a visit? I'm in 'A' wing. I'll get your name down on the approved visitors list. Is there any chance you can come this Sunday, say at 2pm? I need to see you as soon as possible.'

'Yes, Tim, of course I will. I'll be there. Is there anything you need?'

'Yes, there is actually. Can you please bring in the jeans, trainers, socks, underwear and polo shirts I left with you? You know, the ones I left in that small suitcase.'

'Yes, that's no problem, Tim. Do you need anything else, such as books or writing material or anything?'

Before Tim could respond to Alan, the call was silenced by the signal of the end of Association by the sound of the loud ringing of a brass bell. Almost immediately came the bellowing of commands by prison officers for inmates to return to their cells.

Tim replaced the receiver. At least he'd got through to Alan and now at last he could start to work out the first steps in his plan to escape.

***

DS Holdsworth and Jean Price were busy making a start on building their case data. They now had the list of prisoners held in HMP Dinas Bay that were originally from the Midshire Police area. The list had been handed to Jean in order to capture the appropriate force records and store them in the XIM database. There were some forty-five in total, at least eleven of which were lifers who had been moved from various Category A prisons. But the majority were serving sentences of up to ten years. Jean set about recording the data and making any additional notes on each prisoner from the crime and intelligence system.

'I know it's early days yet, Jean, but can you spot anything through the Link Analysis charts? For example whether there are any likely gang connections amongst this lot?'

'Too early to say just yet, sarge, as I haven't loaded all the data. There are one or two prisoners who are known to each other prior to conviction but that's about all. Once I've downloaded all the crime and intelligence data for these I should at least see possible connections. Of course the past data won't necessarily highlight what is being planned in there. Strange sort of case this as, of course, we haven't as yet had a crime or an incident as such to investigate. It's a bit different to what I've been working on in the past.'

'That's right, Jean! Welcome to the world of local intelligence, where something that might not seem important now could very well be paramount later on! But I guess your National Intelligence training course would have covered all that.'

'Yes, it did indeed. I tell you what I have spotted though. Do you remember the arrests of the joint investigation we worked on involving card fraud and identity theft earlier this year?'

'Yeah. What of it?' replied the DS, who was now busy reading through the pages of convictions. 'I shouldn't think any of that lot would be involved.'

'Well, two of the offenders, Ridgway and Ellis, are in prison there!'

CHAPTER 7

Tim and Charlie were minding their own business as they strolled casually around the exercise yard when suddenly they were approached from behind by Higson.

'Afternoon Posh Boy, settled in with your boyfriend have we, must be nice and cosy in that cell?' sneered Higson, who had decided to accompany them on their exercise circuit.

'Push off, Higson, go and pester someone else,' replied Charlie, quickening the pace.

'And you will do what exactly if I don't?' came the sneering reply.

Tim remained silent while they came to a sudden halt and Charlie stood up to Higson, who was now face to face with him, almost breathing into him. The other inmates continued to walk around or gather in huddles unaware of the confrontation. The prison officers however were keeping a watchful eye on them.

'You'll find out Higson, now look pal we are not interested in whatever it is you or your cronies are after, so push off, crawl back under your stone or wherever you have come from and leave us alone.'

'I'm just curious to know if you pair would be interested in any stuff, you know, I'm the man, speed, coke, brown you know the score, I can get it for you easy enough, just give me the word.'

'We are not interested Higson so sod off, when will you get it into your thick head we don't do drugs, so go and find someone else to play with,' replied Charlie as they continued their walk around the perimeter.

'It's never too late to start guys, look there's no pressure, I can even do you a free sample, call it a trial offer if you like, just remember I'm your man,' said Higson. 'Oh, but there was something else that I wanted to discuss with you pair, a little bird tells me that you or Posh Boy here might have some skills that we could very well be interested in?'

'Oh and what skills would those be, Higson? No, let me guess, let me see now, yes I'm now a dab hand at washing up and Tim here knows a thing or two about ironing in laundries,' laughed Charlie, nodding over to Tim who was grinning.

'Very funny Ellis, hilarious, you should be on the stage you know, I'm pissing myself laughing as you can see,' replied Higson, who was now losing his patience somewhat. 'No, the skills I'm looking for would be computing skills, we could use these in return for various favours if you get my drift?'

'Well, we are not interested, you can take your drift and shove it up your arse Higson, now sod off. Come on Tim ignore him, there's a nasty smell around here.'

To Tim's surprise he'd never seen Charlie behave like this before and realised that really this was the only way to deal with some of these bullies. Higson cleared off and re-joined his mates who were now gathered in a corner.

'How on earth did Higson know about my computer skills?' said Tim.

'Oh, it doesn't take them long, they make it their business to know your background, they probably know more about you than you do.'

After the hooter had gone and when they eventually returned to their cell Tim was surprised to see an envelope on his bed; he recognised the handwriting.

The envelope had already been opened but that was standard practice in the prison, the prison officers didn't have time to read them but just needed to check that certain items were not enclosed.

'I see you have had post, Tim,' said Charlie, who was curious and at the same time quite envious. 'No one writes to me or even visits me, my family don't even seem to want to know me anymore.'

'I'm sure they will visit you soon Charlie, perhaps you should write to them?' said Tim as he started to read the letter.

'Well I wrote a couple of weeks ago but I haven't received anything back yet, anyway who is it from? No, don't tell me you've won the lottery and the money will be earning interest while you are in here you jammy bugger.'

'I wish, no it's from Alan at the Jelly Bean café, he's coming to see me this Sunday, here have a read,' replied Tim as he passed the letter to Charlie.

Mr Timothy Ridgway
c/o HMP Dinas Bay
'A' Wing
Gwynedd
North Wales

Dear Tim,
Thanks for your phone call the other day, it was really good to hear from you.

Like you I was really saddened to hear the sentence you were given but knowing you as I do I'm sure you will be just somehow making the best of the situation.

I would love to come and visit you at HMP Dinas Bay. I can always get someone to look after the café so I've made arrangements to come over Sunday 15th November as discussed and I will bring those items of clothing you were after. Please ring me again if for some reason you are not allowed visitors. The café is quiet this time of year as you can imagine so I may even close it for the day. It's a good drive from here and I'm somewhat surprised they placed you further away, I would have thought you would be in one of the Liverpool or Manchester prisons, anyway it's no problem and I'll definitely come over, Sundays as it happens are the best days for me so if you can please arrange a visiting order I'll be over.

Have you heard where Charlie and Tariq ended up?

Best regards

Alan

'Well, that's fantastic news Tim, you'll have to update him although I've no idea where Tariq ended up and I don't really care to be quite honest,' said Charlie, handing back the letter, who clearly had a dislike for Tariq. 'It was his own stupid fault getting arrested trying to pass himself off as someone else in a bank, he's a complete tosser if you ask me.'

***

The following day Tim Ridgway was busy with his laundry duties, this involved him working as part of a small team of inmates who collected the white net laundry bags from all those in every wing. The HMP Dinas Bay prison had been selected to trial a method of laundry processing not always found in other prisons. Each of the five wings had a designated laundry day which kept the Laundry guys busy from Monday to Friday. Every prisoner was issued with a laundry bag which contained a tag with his name and cell number.

This was for the prisoner's private clothing; prison issued equipment such as bedsheets, etc. were all dealt with separately. Each day straight after breakfast Tim and his workmates would collect the bags from that particular wing and spend all day processing them.

A set number of these bags would be washed together in each washing machine at the same time and then dried in the large industrial tumble driers. It was not ideal and it was a huge job but nevertheless well organised. The bags then had to be returned to the relevant cells later the same day unopened with the contents washed and dried so in theory items of clothing shouldn't really get lost but on occasion they did.

After a hard day Tim had just returned all the bags to the cells on his own wing and returned to his own cell exhausted. Charlie was working late in the kitchen and Tim had just sat down on his bed to read the newspaper when the bell rang for Association. He decided he'd make his way down the corridor into the communal area; he followed the line of inmates and went in and took a seat in the corner. He watched as a betting tournament started on the pool table and a large number of inmates sat down to watched an afternoon antiques program on the TV.

He thought it odd that even in prison some of the inmates would educate themselves on valuable antiques in readiness for their release. All he needed now was a quiet session just to sit down and relax on his own reading the newspaper after a hard day's work. Suddenly the room darkened somewhat and he felt the presence of a small gathering surrounding him, it was Higson and three of his mates. Without any warning Higson kicked off, 'Eh Posh Boy, what have you done with my socks?'

'Are you talking to me, Higson?' said Tim, putting down his newspaper.

'You're the only posh boy around here, I can't see anyone else around here, can you boys?'

Higson's mates all laughed and nodded in agreement.

'I haven't a clue what you are bloody talking about Higson? Why on earth would I be interested in your bloody socks, now sod off and leave me alone in peace. I've had a hard day's work and I just need to relax,' said Tim, trying to ignore him and continuing to read the newspaper.

'Ah diddums, what a shame, did you hear that lads, he's had a hard day's work, Posh Boy here has had a busy day, ah bless!'

Tim continued reading his paper and tried to ignore them until Higson started to lose his temper.

'Look here sunshine, I put a pair of my best socks in the washing bag and you've bloody well lost them. You owe me Posh Boy, big style so how exactly are you going to repay me?'

'Sod off Higson why don't you go and pick on someone else, I haven't seen your bloody socks but if I do come across them rest assured I'll bin them!'

Just then Higson grabbed hold of Tim by the throat and pushed him up out of his seat and pinned him against the wall with his right knee firmly pushed into Tim's groin. Tim felt Higson's hands tighten around his throat and he was struggling to breathe. He could smell Higson's foul stinking breath. There were no prison officers in sight but in any case Higson's mates had already shielded him and a small crowd had also gathered around to watch.

'You don't seem to understand, Posh Boy, this is a warning, it's a caution, you owe me ok, just watch your step, you won't always have your mate Charlie Ellis to look after you. So take this as a warning and if I was you I'd keep looking to see who is behind you.'

Just then Higson loosened his grip and pushed Tim back into his seat, the small crowd dispersed and Tim was left panting and trying to catch his breath.

CHAPTER 8

Sunday 15th November. 2015

'We'll miss you, Dad,' said Tom, as he hugged his father. Tom was Jack Hodgson's only son, he had just turned thirteen and he was trying hard to hold back his tears. 'I hate it when you go away, you will write to me Dad, won't you? Promise me you will write.'

'Yes, of course I will and I'll miss you too. I'll write to you all, now don't you worry Tom, it will soon go I promise. I'll also try and call you on the phone whenever I can. Don't forget you are the man in charge of the house now while I'm away so I'm relying on you to look after everyone,' replied Jack Hodgson as he loaded his bags into the boot of the car.

'I miss you too, daddy, will you bring me something back?' said Emily, who was stretching up and not really having a full understanding of time or the situation.

Jack picked up Emily, his only daughter, who was ten years old, and gave her a huge hug.

'I will miss you too Emily, come on now, let's have one last kiss or I'll be late. Now you both look after your mummy while I'm away and both of you be on your very best behaviour ok?'

'We will daddy, we will,' replied Emily.

'Look after yourself love, and ring us to let us know that you are ok,' said Sue, who had been putting on a brave face and was also now starting to choke up.

'Goodbye love, goodbye all, I'll be in touch as often as I can,' said Jack as he closed the car door. He started the ignition, gave one last wave, he couldn't bring himself to look back and drove off wondering when the next time would be when they would be reunited as a family again.

He then drove to the second-hand car dealer as arranged, picked up the keys of the Vauxhall Astra, exchanged the bags from his Volvo estate, locked everything up and drove off in the direction of Conway down the M56 and onto the A55.

***

Alan Smith decided to drive over to the prison on the Sunday afternoon; he'd thought about catching the train and whilst it was a good service from Manchester to get near there he would have had to get a taxi and spend the night in a hotel as there were no suitable return services. He elected therefore to drive. He set out mid-morning and arrived just as the prison gates were opening for visiting. He checked in with the prison officer that was on duty, who checked the list and confirmed the visiting order was in place. Tim would be seated on table 17. Alan was then searched and took his place in the queue in the visiting waiting room. It was a sad scene indeed to see young wives and children being screened and waiting patiently to see their loved ones. Once in he made his way to the right table, he noticed that every table had just three seats with one being a different colour to the other two seats. The prisoners always sat on the red seats. Minutes later Tim appeared wearing a bright red prison issue vest, he'd lost weight and looked very gaunt, he was pale and drawn and it shocked Alan, who decided it was best not saying anything in case it upset Tim.

'Hi Tim, how are you, it's good to see you after all this time, you are not looking too bad,' said Alan, standing up to shake his hand.

'Hi Alan, well I must admit I'm not really used to manual labour but thanks ever so much for coming over to see me, I really appreciate it, did you have a safe journey across here?'

'Not bad at all really, a few Sunday drivers dawdling as you can imagine, but yes a nice drive over here to be honest. Be a bit different in the summer with lots of holidaymakers I imagine. Anyway how are they treating you?'

'Oh, not bad I suppose, when I think about it I've been really lucky, I'm sharing a cell with Charlie, I mean what are the chances of that happening?'

'Amazing, I wondered where he would have ended up. There's no news on Tariq, I don't suppose?'

'No, no idea, he could be in here for all I know, maybe in another wing.'

'Look Alan, I need to ask you a big favour,' said Tim suddenly lowering his voice.

'Yes of course, you've done enough for me over the years, what is it?' replied Alan leaning closer.

'Well, I need for you to arrange a visit for me, I need you to ask Father O'Brien from St. Mary's Church, you know the church on West Street, to come over to see me as soon as possible, it must be Father O'Brien do you understand?'

'Are you going all religious or something and why Father O'Brien of all people, don't you have a visiting vicar here you could talk to?'

'Yes there is a prison chaplain and no I'm not going religious but I can't explain here, look can you do that for me, it must be Father O'Brien.'

'Yes, of course I will, but why Father O'Brien all of a sudden,' said Alan, who was now clearly puzzled by the request.

'Look I can't go into detail, it has to be him. Do you remember the laptop I used to leave back at your café, you know the one I used to sort out some of the virus and hacking attempts you experienced in the cafe?'

'Yes, what of it, it's still there, I keep it locked up in the cupboard.'

'Well I want you to scan a note in and copy it onto the hard drive of that laptop. I'm going to give you a note when you leave, just run the contents of the note through the program called "*Jellybean-unscramble.exe*" and it will explain my plan. I'll also be in touch by text,' whispered Tim.

'I didn't know you were allowed any mobiles in prison, a text?' exclaimed Alan.

'Hush, keep your voice down, you're right we are not allowed mobiles but I know where I can get access to one, you will get a text from me as well so please follow the instructions to the letter.'

'Is there anything else you would like me to send into the prison, clothing, that sort of thing, I've already dropped off those other items you asked for, presumably that all gets checked?'

'Well like I mentioned before I badly need jeans, polo shirts, that sort of thing but I could do with my electric razor, the cheap wet ones here are cutting me to ribbons. You've got a spare key to my apartment, you should find everything you need in there.'

'Are you allowed to have an electric razor?'

'Yeah, that's one of the few electrical items you can send me apparently.'

'Ok, will do, I'll bundle them up and get a parcel sent in.'

They continued to talk about how the café business was going and after about an hour the bell went which signalled the end of visiting time. Alan got up to shake hands with Tim and as he did he felt something slip inside the farewell handshake. He immediately placed his hand in his pocket and deposited the note safely.

'Cheerio Tim, I'll be in touch, you look after yourself,' said Alan as he waved goodbye and left the prison.

***

DC Jack Hodgson had a trouble-free drive over to the Lleyn Peninsula with no hold ups. It was a beautiful autumn day for driving, warm for the time of year with not a cloud in the sky. The colours of autumn were simply spectacular with leaves now falling from the trees sometimes completely covering the road in front of him. He decided as he was in no hurry to get there to travel instead across country roads. He left the A55 at Dobshill and made his way through the old pottery town of Buckley. A town he'd grown up in and had so many wonderful childhood memories. The potteries had long gone now replaced by modern housing estates. He continued onward passing through the delightful villages of Afon-Wen and Bodfari alongside the Clwydian Hills.

The drive was breath taking with glorious views of Mother Nature's autumn foliage in fine display en-route.

After passing through St. Asaph, Jack had now re-joined the A55 dual carriage-way which hugged the spectacular coastline and he'd decided to stop for a short break after passing through the Penmaenbach tunnel. He bought himself a coffee from a tea bar in one of the many laybys and sat on a wall overlooking the Menai Straits across to Beaumaris on the island of Anglesey; to his right was the huge Great Orme at Llandudno and immediately in front of him was Puffin Island. He was very familiar with this part of the world, having spent many delightful holidays with the family. His thoughts kept returning to his wife and family who he had left behind and wondered when would be the next time he would see them again. He thought this old covert surveillance lark was fine if you are single but no fun for a married man, particularly if you are away indefinitely for months on end. He promised himself this had to be his last undercover mission, it was time for someone else, someone younger and fitter to carry these out, yes he would definitely refuse next time. He opened his briefing pack and re-read his instructions, everything was clear and well documented. In the pack was an HMP ID card with his photograph and his new identity details. He was delighted that Jean Price would be his liaison officer and looked forward to contacting her once he was settled. In the meantime just as any actor would do he had to get himself firmly into character, no longer was he DC Jack Hodgson of Midshire Police but from this moment on until his return home he was John Hughes, a prison officer in HMP security.

It was now gradually turning dusk and with the light fading fast he decided he had better get a move on and check in at the Caravan Park which was much further away than he had first thought. After a drive through narrow twisting lanes and guided only by his faithful sat-nav he eventually arrived at the Min-Y-Coed Caravan Park. He pulled into the new arrivals layby, parked up and made his way across the gravel pathway to the office. He switched on the small torch he had with him, there were signs everywhere, *No parking, No noise after 10pm, No ball games, No speeding, No more than 10 miles per hour, No dogs, No visitor's cars past this point* etc etc. He thought to himself I wonder why there isn't a sign which says '*No enjoying yourself*'. The door was locked but he could see a dim light through the dusty venetian blinds on the window. He peered through the gap in the blinds but there appeared to be no one in the office. He rang the doorbell but there was no answer and then he panicked, he suddenly had visions of trying to find a hotel for the night or, worse still, kipping down in the car. He was due into work at eight am the following morning, what if he turned up bedraggled after sleeping in the car, it would not be a good start. It was now dark and there were no streetlights, he walked around the back of the office but everywhere was locked up, an old 1970s Morris van, which looked as though it was ready for the scrapyard, had been abandoned and was parked down the side.

He tried one more time ringing the bell and knocking the door but there was no response, he was about to get back in his car when he spotted a torch light wavering in the distance, he decided to wait for it to get nearer and as it did so out of the darkness came a gravelly voice in a strong Welsh accent.

'Is that you, Mr Hughes, I was told to expect you this afternoon?'

'Erm yes it's me, John Hughes, I'm sorry I am late but I got stuck in traffic I'm afraid,' said Jack Hodgson, lying on both counts. 'I have a static caravan booked with yourself, I paid three months in advance on the telephone last week, I assume I'm in the right place?'

Just then the weathered face behind the voice came into full view, an old man who must have been in his eighties wearing a flat cloth cap, wellingtons and a hole-ridden dirty old boiler suit which had certainly seen some action in its day.

'Yes, you are son, you are certainly in the right place and a fine time to arrive if I may say so. I've been waiting in all afternoon for you, still you're here now that's the main thing. I'll get you the keys to your caravan and then I can shoot off back home, oh my name is Edward Jones by the way, I own the camp site,' came the grumpy response.

'Pleased to meet you Mr Jones, yes I'm sorry once again for keeping you waiting.'

Edward Jones mumbled something as he opened up the office and switched on the main fluorescent light. He hobbled over to an old oak cupboard in the corner which housed a large number of keys on hooks and took a small bunch.

'These are your caravan keys, Mr Hughes. It's on plot 27 down the left hand side, you'll find instructions on everything from lighting, heating and cooking in the top drawer in the kitchen,' he said, handing over the keys, 'I hope you enjoy your stay with us.'

'Thank you Mr Jones, I'm sure everything will be just fine.'

'If you need me in an emergency the telephone number is in the caravan, I'm off now as I'm late for my supper as it is, the toilet block is all locked up for the winter but that shouldn't bother you as you have your own facilities. Just remember no wild parties and please keep to the one way system around the caravan site, we don't want any accidents.'

And before Jack Hodgson could even think about asking any questions the old man had switched the lights off, locked up and in a cloud of black smoke was off down the lane in the old van which had been parked at the side of the office.

Jack drove cautiously round to plot 27 (sticking rigorously to the speed limit and one way system), it was quite obvious he was the only one staying on the entire site, after all it was the middle of November.

The caravan site to Jack's surprise was well laid out in a pleasantly landscaped park in a lightly wooded environment and each caravan was screened with mature hedgerows. Jack continued to drive deep into the unlit campsite and there it was around the bend on a large corner plot, the static caravan on plot 27. The caravan had seen better days, and had probably in its time provided endless summer holidays for families, over many decades. He parked up alongside, went over and unlocked the caravan. As he entered the caravan the first thing that hit him was the smell of damp. He fumbled for the light switch and having found it he was pleasantly surprised to see how clean and tidy it was inside, in fact it was immaculate. He thought, so this is home for the next three months or even longer, well at least I've got everything I need here. He turned on the heating, switched on the TV and went out to get his bags from the car. With his arms full he unloaded the bags in the main bedroom where he unpacked his belongings and filled the wardrobe and drawers. He'd brought enough provisions to keep him going for the first week. He decided he would use the second bedroom as an office of sorts. He closed the curtains and immediately set about installing and checking out his secure laptop. He plugged in the mobile dongle and checked out the strength of the signal; surprisingly on where he was in the middle of woodland he had a very good signal. Jack logged into the cloud portal, satisfied the security checks of retina, fingerprint and password login and sent the following message which was sent encrypted.

Hi Eagle, everything fine, the Lion sleeps tonight, Nos Da, Lion.

He logged off, poured himself a beer from his survival pack that he'd brought with him, sat back and thought the wild parties will just have to wait for now.

CHAPTER 9

Monday 16th November, 2015

Jean Price arrived in the CID office on the Monday morning, fresh but somewhat tired after a very relaxing weekend with friends away in the Lake District.

'Did you have a good weekend, Jean?' enquired DS Holdsworth, who was busy sifting through his post on his desk.

'Great, thanks sarge, a girls weekend being pampered in a spa hotel in the Lake District, good food, good wine and good company, fantastic, got back late last night, bit tired this morning though. I could have done with another hour in bed this morning.'

'Well it all starts today Jean, although I don't really expect much as it's the Lion's first day in the job. I've been thinking we may possibly get some form of a communication from him later this evening.'

'Yes, I've been thinking how he would be getting on, there was me sitting in a jacuzzi sipping champagne yesterday afternoon and he'd be just getting used to his static caravan. I hope he's ok.'

'Oh, he'll be fine alright, he's a survivor, he's probably already worked out where the best pubs are in the area. I suppose to be honest we won't really hear from him now until later in the week.'

Jean logged into her email and noticed she had a notification waiting for her on the secure cloud portal.

'I think we've already heard from him, Sarge, I'll just check the message queue!'

'Yes, here it is, it's a bit brief but at least we know he's there safely,' said Jean, turning the screen around to DS Holdsworth.

'Great, his first message, hang on what's '*Nos Da*' mean?' enquired the puzzled DS as he read the message.

'Oh, he's picking up the Welsh language already, he's saying goodnight to me,' replied Jean.

***

John Hughes aka Jack Hodgson aka Lion had had one of the best night's sleep he'd ever had; as soon as he'd switched the lights off in the caravan it was pitch black with no road noise or streetlights and just the sound of the wind swirling in the trees around him. He had slept soundly in his bed until the alarm went off at 6.30 am. He made his way into the small bathroom and after fiddling with the temperamental hot water tap managed to take a hot shower. After a quick breakfast of tea and toast he got changed into his prison officer's uniform. He looked at himself up and down in the mirror and thought how it reminded him of his uniform days before he went into CID. He sat down at the table and looked at the map of the area, working out his best route to HMP Dinas Bay.

The short drive to the prison was as predicted, a pleasant drive taking him down through country lanes with only the odd tractor to hold him up but the delay would be nothing compared to the drive he'd been accustomed to in the rush hour period at Midshire Police Divisional HQ.

He arrived at Dinas Bay just prior to 7.45 am, parked the old Vauxhall Astra in the staff car park and walked across to the main gatehouse.

'Bore Da, good morning sir, how can I help you?' said the prison officer cheerily.

'Good morning, my name is John Hughes, I've transferred from HMP Exeter House, this is my first day here. Can you please direct me to Mr Tom Fletcher in the Security Department?' said John, showing the ID card he'd been given in his briefing pack.

'Welcome to Dinas Bay, John, yes I have your name on the list right here, we are expecting you, if you make your way over to the staff entrance just to the right of the visitors sign I am sure they will assist you and we are glad to have you on the team.'

John Hughes thanked the officer and made his way over to the staff entrance. There was no one to be seen and he was just about to ring the bell when an attractive blonde prison officer in her mid-thirties came to the office window.

'Good morning, can I help you sir?'

John flashed his ID card at the window. 'Yes, good morning, I'm from HMP Exeter House, the name is…'

'Ah yes, it's John isn't it, I'm pleased to meet you, I'm Helen Morris. I shall be working with you in Security. I'm just helping out on the front desk at present, yes we are expecting you and a very big welcome to Dinas Bay. I'll just inform our head of department, Tom Fletcher, that you are here,' said Helen Morris, picking up the telephone and dialling the head of security.

'Good morning sir, the new security officer, John Hughes, has arrived and is waiting at the staff reception office. Very well, I'll send him straight through.'

'You can now come through John, Mr Fletcher will meet you at the other side, I'll press the buzzer for you, can you step forward please.'

The electronic glass door slid open and John Hughes made his way into the security vacuum. Once he was inside the electronic door glided shut behind him and as soon as it had closed a few seconds later the glass door on the opposite wall opened up.

He stepped out and took a seat in the small waiting area. Minutes later he was greeted by the Head of Security – Tom Fletcher, a burly no-nonsense silver-haired man who had to be at least six foot six inches tall. Tom Fletcher had been in the prison service for over twenty years and worked his way through the ranks and was surely destined for governor at some point.

'Good morning John, I'm Tom Fletcher, welcome to HMP Dinas Bay, I've heard a lot about you. May I say it's good to have you on board. Walk this way and I'll introduce you to the rest of our team in security. But first, and I'm sure you understand, you must be searched, it's policy of course, I am sure you must be used to this procedure.'

'Good morning sir, yes I quite understand, I'm very used to this,' replied John.

At that point a prison officer suddenly appeared, armed with a check list, from behind a partition wall.

'I just need to carry out a few security checks,' he said efficiently as he ushered John to the table in front of the body scanner, 'but firstly I need to ask you a few questions if that's ok?'

'Yes fine, please go ahead.'

'Do you have a mobile phone?'

'No, I've left it in the car.'

'USB memory sticks on you?'

'No.'

'Tablets of any description?'

'Do you mean iPads or medical ones?'

'Both.'

'No.'

'Lighters?'

'No, I don't smoke.'

On completion of the body search and passing through the security scanners John Hughes rejoined Tom Fletcher, who was patiently waiting near the next set of security doors.

'It will be good to have a fresh pair of eyes on the team, I'm a firm believer that processes and methods can always be improved on, no matter how good they are. I'm looking forward to having you with us, John, and hopefully you can suggest improvements for that type of thing in the department. I also gather you have been researching biometric access in prisons, I would certainly like to discuss that in more detail with you when we have time.'

At that point John realised he really must swot up on the documents he'd brought with him but hadn't yet read from the Force IT department.

They made their way down a long narrow corridor through a series of locked doors. They walked up two flights of stairs and eventually reached the Security Department which had clearly been purpose built with wide views from a large panoramic glass window over the exercise yard and all secure outdoor areas. The large office had its own adjoining kitchen and a separate office which was reserved for the Head of Security. Alongside one wall was a huge bank of CCTV monitors which were displaying various locations within the prison.

'Good morning everyone, can I introduce you to our new member of the department, John Hughes, who has just transferred and is joining us and will be a welcome addition to our team. He already knows the ropes but can I ask you all to please make him welcome, he's already met Helen at the front desk. John, I suggest for now you help Hywel with the intelligence reports. I'll see you later on and we can have a chat afterwards over a coffee. As I say I'm most interested in your opinions,' said Tom Fletcher, going into his office.

The three security officers came forward in turn and introduced themselves and shook hands, firstly Ian Roberts then Bill Gardner and finally Hywel Jones.

'You'd better have this desk next to mine,' said Hywel, somewhat abrasively, who clearly didn't want to spend any time with John for some reason. 'I suggest for the time being you familiarise yourself with the database here. You can use my login details for now, which are on a yellow post-it note on my screen.'

John couldn't get over how lax the security was at Dinas Bay, sharing usernames and passwords and, worse still, displaying them for all and sundry to see in the office. He thought how could anyone expect to pass a quality security audit here. He knew from his role years ago as a prison liaison officer that other prisons were certainly not as slack as this but nevertheless he decided he didn't want to rock the boat at this early stage. He sat down and noticed across one of the walls a large whiteboard displaying a hand-written diagram, showing prisoner names and links, it must have taken someone weeks, maybe months, to create. John sat at the terminal, logged in using Hywel's details and proceeded to research the incident and intelligence reports. He couldn't have wished for a better start, soon he'd worked out which wings were the most disruptive and who the key players were. He could have found this out from reading the manually created wall chart of course, but at least the computer system would be more up to date, or so he hoped.

'So what brings you to relocate to this part of the world John?' asked Bill Gardner, who was busy filing documents.

'Well, we have relatives in the area and the wife wanted to get back near to her family, you know how it is. We spent a lot of time on holiday here, beautiful place,' said John, quickly thinking up a story. He somehow hadn't anticipated this and assumed that prison officers transferred on a regular basis.

'So whereabouts do the relatives of your family live then?'

'Oh, erm, Llanrwst way,' replied John as quick as he could, thinking of one of the road signs he'd seen on the way over yesterday.

'Is that right, amazing, what a coincidence, my wife has relatives over there, who knows we might even be related, well it is a small world. I bet I know the family,' said Bill Gardner enthusiastically.

Much to John's relief Bill's phone rang at that moment and he had to take the call, otherwise he felt the conversation could be getting somewhat out of control. John Hughes thought to himself I really must work out some background here and get it clear in my mind.

***

Tim and Charlie were playing cards during Association in the community area when Tim noticed one particular prisoner who always seemed to be on his own and never seemed to mix with anyone. Tim thought he recognised him from somewhere so he stopped playing for a minute and went over to him.

'Excuse me, I'm sorry to bother you but where have we met before? Did you arrive here from court the same time as me?' said Tim, feeling somewhat sorry for him.

'Yes, that's right last Monday, I wasn't sure it was you, I thought I recognised you, you checked in at the same time,' came the reply.

'Yes of course, that's it, you were the smartly-dressed man in the grey suit, the name's Tim Ridgway,' said Tim, holding out his hand.

'Alan Oldbury,' came the reply, 'so what are you in here for?'

'Oh, fraud and identity theft, I got ten years, and you?'

'Fraud, I got five years for swindling two million out of my boss's company. I was an accountant in the firm and it seemed easy money, it started just as a one-off when I was short of a bob or two but it grew out of hand. I'd just set up a few fictitious companies, produced a few invoices every so often and the rest was easy. It was like a drug, I couldn't resist it.'

'Bloody 'ell, two million, what on earth did you spend that on?'

'That was just it, I needed the money just to pay off my gambling debts, it was a case of in one hand and straight out of the other. I've lost everything now, my house, my wife, the kids, my friends, the whole caboodle.'

'I was going to ask you to come over and have a game of cards with us but I'm not sure we can cope with stakes that high,' said Tim, chuckling to himself, 'anyway come on over and let me introduce you to Charlie.'

They both went over and Tim introduced Alan to Charlie.

'So how come you're here then, Charlie?' enquired Alan, having just relayed his offences.

'Same as Tim really, well almost anyway, I got banged up for fraud and identity theft, nothing like the value of yours of course.'

***

John Hughes had just finished his first day as a security officer in HMP Dinas Bay; he signed out, returned the set of keys he had been given, exchanged it with the key tally at the main staff desk and made his way over to the car park. He'd had a reasonably good first day, he'd already worked out who the known troublemakers were in the prison, well the inmates at least, and he had started to research some of the individuals from his own force area.

Just before finishing for the day he'd been given a short tour of the prison by Tom Fletcher and he was impressed with the design and how modern the whole building was compared to some of the old Victorian ones, which were still being used and gradually replaced across the UK. He'd been less impressed, however, with one or two of his fellow prison officers in the department he was working in.

The sea fog was now closing in fast as he drove out of the car park and he hoped his sat nav would guide him back to the caravan site as he clearly hadn't yet got used to the route. He decided he would get as close to the caravan park as possible and try and locate a couple of nearby hostelries. He was badly in need of a drink and with only a few hundred yards to go before he arrived at the caravan site he found a delightful country pub – The Smithy Arms, a traditional pub which over the years had lost none of its old charm. It was just a walk down the lane from the caravan park, it was ideal. He decided to drive back to the caravan site first so he could get changed out of his uniform and walk back and have a few pints. He parked his car, had a quick change of clothes and walked back down the lane to the pub. He walked into the oak-beamed bar and was immediately offered a warm welcome by the hosts Julia and Steve. The pub was definitely quite a find. He was spoilt for choice from a list of superbly kept real ales brewed locally. The pub was ideal with good old fashioned friendly service in a place absolutely loaded with character.

It was quiet as it was early doors with just the odd local sitting at the bar and John wondered how they managed to make a living in such a rural area with so few customers. John took a seat in the corner, opened up his newspaper with his back to a roaring log fire. This is it, he thought, this will do nicely. I've found my base for the next few months and all within a stone's throw of the caravan.

After a hearty meal of steak and chips washed down with several pints later he decided he'd better make his way back to the caravan to report his initial findings back to HQ. To his surprise the fog had lifted but it was now emptying down with rain and he had not brought even a raincoat or umbrella.

The caravan park was in darkness and he switched on his torch to avoid tripping in the many potholes in the approach road which were now starting to fill with rainwater. As he approached the office at the entrance he thought he heard voices but there was no light on or sign of anyone. He stopped, waited and listened, he couldn't hear anything, so he walked on a bit further through the pouring rain when suddenly without any warning, out from behind a caravan, appeared the figure of Edward Jones, the campsite owner. Gone was the flat cap, which had now been replaced by a dripping wet sou'wester.

'Nasty night Mr Hughes, only an idiot would be out on a night like this. Have you settled in, I trust you have everything you need?'

'Erm, yes thanks Mr Jones, you gave me quite a shock there, I didn't expect to see you out in this weather.'

'Just doing a quick security check, as you well know, you can't be too careful you know this time of year, well I'll say goodnight then,' replied Edward Jones as he disappeared into the darkness.

'Goodnight Mr Jones.'

John Hughes thought, did I imagine that or does he know more about me than I think he does. He was glad to get into his caravan, he switched the lights on, turned the heating on, dried himself off and locked the door.

He switched on his laptop and started working on his first surveillance report.

CHAPTER 10

'Has he made contact with us yet?'

'Yes, he's settled in, it's early days yet, we expect to have an initial report from him later this week.'

'Good, keep me informed of any developments, I don't want any of this to go tits up and he could be in serious trouble if his cover is blown. If it does get messy we must get him out of there as soon as possible, alright?'

'Understood, sir.'

***

'Is that Father O'Brien?'

'It is and who am I speaking to?'

'Oh, good evening Father, my name is Alan Smith from the Jelly Bean cafe. I am sorry to ring you late at night but I'm ringing with regard to a good friend of mine who unfortunately has fallen on bad times. You may remember him, his name is Tim Ridgway, he used to attend your church regularly with his parents Alison and Michael Ridgway.'

'Oh yes I remember Tim, he lost his parents in that hit and run accident several years ago. Very sad, I wondered where he had ended up, a nice young man who showed a lot of promise as I recall, is he alright?'

'Yes, he's alright although I'm afraid to say he is currently serving a prison sentence for fraud and identity theft. He was wondering whether you could possibly come over and visit him in prison?'

'Yes of course I will, the Ridgways were a lovely family, regular church goers, they would do anything for anyone. I'm so sorry to hear that he has ended up in prison, which prison is he in, presumably Manchester?'

'No, I'm afraid he's a little further afield than that, he's in HMP Dinas Bay on the North Wales coast.'

'Is he indeed, well that's quite a way to travel but yes I can probably get over there, it will give me a good reason to visit my sister while I'm over in that part of the world.'

'Great, I'll tell Tim you can make it then, I believe visiting is Saturdays and Sundays between 2pm and 3.30pm.'

'Well I'm afraid Sunday is out of the question of course for me but yes, I can get over there next Saturday, will you please pass the message onto him?'

'I will indeed Father, he'll be delighted to see you and thank you ever so much for your time, I know Tim will really appreciate your visit. If there is any problem visiting I'll call you back.'

Alan then replaced the telephone. He powered up Tim's laptop and connected it to his own printer/scanner. He then scanned the handwritten note in that Tim had given him, it was neatly set out in block letters but made no sense whatsoever. He loaded it into the program called *"jellybean-unscramble.exe"*, pressed the decrypt button and immediately up on the screen came the readable message.

Alan at first looked puzzled with what he read in front of him, he read it again and then smiled, suddenly he knew exactly what he had to do next.

***

Tuesday 17th November, 2015

Jean Price had just created the first link analysis chart from the prisoner data and was in discussion over it with DS Holdworth.

'So talk me through this Jean, what is it exactly that I am looking at here?' said DS Holdsworth, opening up the chart window on his desktop.

'Well, sarge, you will see that I've created a fresh database and loaded in the data for just those prisoners, their offences and connections from the Midshire Police area. As we receive fresh information coming in from Dinas Bay or any other sources for that matter these charts will be updated automatically of course. You will see that we do have some connections already but you would expect that; for example here you can see that certain prisoners are already connected through their previous involvement in the same crime reports,' said Jean, pointing to a cluster of objects within the chart.

'Excellent, yes I recognise one or two names in there, let's hope we get something from the Lion's initial report in the next few days.'

***

John Hughes arrived at the prison early that morning; he signed in at reception, exchanged his tally for the set of prison keys, passed swiftly through the security check and headed upstairs to the office. As he entered the office he was greeted by Helen Morris, who was in the kitchen on her own.

'Good morning John, this lot never seem to wash their mugs after them, I hope they are a bit tidier at home. I'm just about to make a brew, what do you fancy?' she said, as she prepared the mugs and switched on the kettle.

'Good Morning Helen, yes I'm quite parched, I'd love a brew, I'll have a coffee with two sugars please,' he replied, as he settled down at his desk.

'So, how long have you worked in the prison service, Helen?'

'Well I'm one of the new ones John, I used to work for the local council in their Housing Repairs department and when they built this place and I saw the job adverts, I thought, why not, I fancy a change of career, I could have a go at that.'

'So are you enjoying it?'

'Yes, it's certainly different from what I've been used to, a bit different from people complaining about their houses.'

'I can imagine.'

'So John, have you found your way around here yet, how does it compare to your last prison?'

John thought hard and stroked his beard, he remembered from the conversations he'd had with the real John Hughes on the pros and cons of HMP Exeter House.

'Oh, I'm not sure I could find my way around here just yet but this place is fantastic I have to say compared to the last prison. You can see it's been designed and purpose-built, it's what a prison should be. The last place was a nightmare I can tell you, it was built in 1844 and we regularly had issues with violence and drugs particularly with the layout of the prison, you could hide anything or anyone in there. I lost count of the escape attempts. To be quite honest it was out of date and completely overcrowded. I'll tell you this though, the sooner it's replaced by one of these modern prisons the better.'

'Well we do have those issues here as well I'm afraid, from time to time, even the modern prisons can't prevent that,' replied Helen, as she placed a mug of coffee in front of him. 'I must leave you I'm afraid as I'm covering again on the staff entry window, I'll see you later on.'

Helen left the office and minutes later the door swung open and in marched Hywel Jones, followed by Bill Gardner.

Hywel Jones went over to his desk and didn't say a word, he logged in and pulled out a pile of intelligence reports from his desk drawer, he seemed somehow more depressed than ever this morning.

'Good morning all,' said Bill, as he hung his coat up on the rack behind the door. 'So how are you today John, starting to feel at home now I guess?'

'I'm fine thanks,' said John, 'well no I wouldn't exactly call it home.'

'No of course not, it was silly of me to think of it like that. Anyway I'm sure you are comfortable with the way we do things around here, pretty much standard with what you did previously, I imagine.'

'Yes, I'm getting there, getting there alright.'

John Hughes took a swig of coffee and logged into the intelligence database using the same username and password belonging to Hywel that he'd been given yesterday. He looked across at Hywel, who looked as miserable as ever.

'I could really do with having my own username and password Hywel, this is not ideal of course using yours, as there is no clear audit trail on which one of us accessed the system.'

'I'll arrange for you to have one allocated,' came the brief reply from Hywel, who was now more deeply engrossed in reading the daily newspaper than sifting through intelligence reports.

'Great, as soon as possible please, Hywel, in the meantime I'll plough on and enter the intelligence reports from the weekend, at least it will make good reading for your own personal efficiency on data entry,' replied John, who was unhappy using someone else's login details, although it did give him the opportunity to search for anything he wished for without it being traced back specifically to him.

Hywel mumbled something, stormed out and clearly didn't appreciate John's comments.

'Bit touchy isn't he, quite a sensitive little character and he doesn't say a lot. He's got a face like a slapped arse this morning,' said John Hughes.

'Oh, I'd take no notice of Hywel, he is very rarely happy, he has a lot on his mind I think with the cost of Christmas coming up and a wife and four kids to support, his mind is on other things. He somehow doesn't seem to appreciate that you have joined the team to help us out. We've been overstretched for months now with an increasing workload and a backlog of intelligence reports to deal with,' replied Bill Gardner, who had set about updating the whiteboard.

'Well the level of reports has certainly gone up this past month, we must try and get to the source of some of these,' said Bill, stepping back from the whiteboard and admiring his handiwork. 'Looks like we're up 45% on the previous month.'

John decided to push on and decided to ignore the Hywel incident, he thought how poor it was to have a system which allowed the same person to login to two different workstations at the same time. He started reading through the pile of reports. There had been over thirty intelligence reports recorded over the previous weekend, some of which were no more than observations on changes of inmate behaviour but it was noticeable that the majority were in 'A' wing. Six intelligence reports were related to fighting and all involved the inmate Arthur Higson, who was clearly a troublemaker. He decided to run a summary report off showing all the reports from all wings for the past three months which involved multiple inmates. He waited until he had the office to himself before printing off the output to avoid arousing any suspicion.

CHAPTER 11

Saturday 21st November, 2015

Father Seamus O'Brien had travelled over to Bangor by train from Manchester the previous day. It was a great opportunity for him to catch up with his sister Siobhan who lived in the nearby village of Menai Bridge. She had met him off the train on the Friday afternoon and he'd enjoyed dinner with the family, chatting about old times and having a relaxing evening. It was rare to get together as a family and he wished he could have stayed for the whole weekend but he had to get back for Sunday services. His sister had kindly driven him across to HMP Dinas Bay the following morning.

The weather had closed in overnight and the gale force winds and the rain made driving conditions exceedingly difficult, particularly down the coast road. They eventually arrived at the prison just in time for visiting. Siobhan waited in the car and Father O'Brien, who was unsteady on his feet, made his way across to the visitors' entrance. He signed in and took his place in the waiting room and waited to be called to be searched prior to entering the actual visiting room. He didn't have to wait long before an officer called out his name.

'Father O'Brien, can you please walk this way,' said the officer, who guided him to the security scanner.

'Please remove your watch, belt and shoes and place them in the tray.'

Father O'Brien did what the officer requested and passed the tray through the scanner. He limped over to the body scanner and immediately on entering it set the alarm off.

'Have you emptied your pockets, Father?' enquired the prison officer.

'Yes, I have nothing on me but I think I know what has triggered that.'

'Yes, and what would that be then?'

'Well, I have a metal plate in my left leg following a very bad motorcycle accident I had a few years ago, I think it could very well be that.'

'Yes, you're probably right Father, it probably is that,' replied the officer, allowing him through and ticking his list off. 'Please take a seat on table 19, you shouldn't have to wait too long.'

Father O'Brien collected his belongings from the tray, tidied himself up after the security inspection and sat down at table 19. Every table was busy with families and friends waiting patiently and the officers had now locked all the entrance doors. Minutes later the doors from the prison itself were opened and the prisoners were allowed in to meet their visitors. Tim Ridgway appeared; he had aged considerably since Father O'Brien last saw him and he smiled when he saw his visitor.

'Hello Father, thank you ever so much for coming over to see me, I really do appreciate it, I cannot thank you enough,' said Tim, shaking his hand.

'Hello Tim, it's a long time no see and I just wished we were meeting under better circumstances, however the main thing is that you are fit and well. How have you been, are they looking after you in here?'

'Yes, I'm as well as can be expected under the circumstances, I'm starting to get used to prison life, which takes some adjusting I can tell you.'

'I'm sure it does, well that's good. I'm so sorry that this has happened to you but you mustn't lose faith, Tim, whatever you do, you will think the whole world is against you at times and sometimes these events are sent to try us, you know you can grow stronger through this. I'm not going to judge you on what you have done. Men have done a lot worse than you have and I'm sure you clearly regret all this happening but look on this as the start of a new future, it's not the end, you won't always be in here. You will look back on this and think I am a better person now for that experience, God will forgive you, have faith in him, Tim.'

'You are right, Father, I won't always be in here and I look forward to starting my life all over again.'

'That's the spirit, Tim, now is there anything I can get you?'

Tim could now detect that one of the prison officers was eavesdropping on the conversation.

'Well, yes there is, Father, could you please send me in a bible?'

'Yes of course, son, I will see what I can arrange.'

***

John Hughes needed to finalise his initial report after completing his first week at HMP Dinas Bay and send it off to DS Holdsworth and Jean Price via the secure portal connection. He'd smuggled out the intelligence summary he'd printed out. There were a number of prisoners who he thought would be of interest, some from the Midshire area and some from North Wales itself. John had the weekend to himself and although he was tempted to return home he decided he had far too much to do and needed to work on his report. He also felt he needed to settle in and explore his new surroundings.

He spent most of the Saturday working in the caravan on the laptop, making notes from the intelligence summary and outlining possible connections. He knew that on Monday morning the team back at Divisional HQ would be waiting to update their database.

Eventually by mid-afternoon he'd collated his information, he uploaded it to the portal and sat back.

It was now time for a well-earned pint or two so after a quick change he locked up and took the short walk to the Smithy Arms. On the way he made a brief phone call from the phone box at the entrance to the caravan site.

**

Tim Ridgway had now returned to his cell after visiting hours, he was pleased that Father O'Brien had come all that way to see him.

As he entered his cell he saw there had been a parcel delivered for him, he could see it had already been opened and examined by prison staff and resealed. Tim hastily opened it and saw to his delight that jeans, tee shirts and his shaver that he had requested had been sent by Alan from the Jelly Bean.

The prisoners were kept occupied in the week days and Saturdays in the prison could be a miserable affair, particularly if a prisoner hadn't had any visitors that weekend.

Charlie was curled up on his bed, once again he hadn't received any visitors and seeing other prisoners going off to the visitors' room had clearly had a detrimental effect on him. Tim could see he was very upset as he entered the cell.

'Still no news from your parents yet, Charlie, I'm sure they'll be in touch?' said Tim, trying his best to cheer Charlie up.

'No, nothing Tim, I think they have disowned me.'

'No, I'm sure they haven't, don't think that Charlie, maybe they haven't come to terms with it all yet and they probably don't wish to see you in here, it's probably too upsetting for them.'

'Yes I realise that, none of my family have ever been in trouble like this and my mother in particular has taken it badly, but it doesn't stop them writing to me does it?'

'Fair point Charlie, but come on, cheer up, you're making me miserable.'

'Yes, I'm sorry, Tim, I'm not very good company at the moment.'

But Tim had other things on his mind, his escape plan, he had no intention of staying longer than need be in prison and at some point soon he needed to discuss this with Charlie.

**

Sue Hodgson had taken the tram into Manchester city centre to do some shopping, the place was packed as usual and parking could have been a bit of a nightmare in the run up to Christmas. She'd left the children behind at home, allowing her plenty of time to get around the city without the distraction of them wanting to go into a fast food restaurant or return home early. Sue's mother had come over to look after Tom and Emily.

The city centre was heaving and the popular Christmas markets were in full flow, hundreds of festive food and gift stalls located in various streets throughout the city offering everything from German and Spanish beer to crafts and jewellery, you name it, it was there on display. She only wished Jack was with her to enjoy it and although she'd received a phone call from him earlier in the week she still didn't know whether or not he would be with them for Christmas. The children were already missing their father and she was doing all she could to keep the family happy and thinking positive.

She had just entered the Arndale Centre when she received a phone call from a phone number she didn't recognise. At first she thought it might be one of those crank calls or someone trying to sell her something, she thought twice about even answering it.

'Sue, it's Jack, I thought I'd give you the good news, I should be home for Christmas Day.'

'Oh, that's fantastic news Jack, the children will be absolutely delighted, I can't wait to get home to tell them.'

'How are they?'

'Oh, they are fine love, they miss you, we all do.'

'And you are coping without me?'

'Yes, we are managing but we badly need you home.'

'It won't be long now, I miss you all love, but I'll be home soon to see you. Love you, I must go.'

CHAPTER 12

Monday 23rd November, 2015

John Hughes had arrived in HMP Dinas Bay early again, he had been so used to getting up early back home and fighting his way through the city traffic. The journey into the prison was delightful, country roads with hardly anyone on them. He was the first one in the office. He logged in again using Hywel Jones's details and started updating the backlog of intelligence reports from the weekend. It was a slow process, firstly having to read each one, research the database for additional notes and then record the actual data but it needed to be done. Having a limited number of staff to record and research slowed the process down even further.

He was just reading through a particular incident relating to a fight on 'B' wing when the Head of Security arrived into the office.

'Good morning John, I'm pleased to see you're an early bird and on with the job in hand. Have you settled in here now?'

'Good morning sir, yes settled in nicely thank you, I couldn't sleep so thought I'd make an early start on this lot,' replied John, pointing to the pile of intelligence reports. 'Do you know it's like painting the Forth road bridge, no sooner are you on top of it than you have to start all over again.'

'Aye, that's right John, I did the job for five years and I know exactly what you mean.'

'We could do with a few more staff really sir, keeping on top of this lot is quite a job.'

'Yes, I agree with you John but our staff keep getting poached by other departments to go and work on the wings, they are desperately short of resources, in fact from today Helen Morris has had to be moved back onto shifts to help them on 'A' wing. Anyway I must go I have to present a report to one of the governors. Keep up the good work and I'm pleased you've settled in so quickly,' said Tom Fletcher as he left the office.

John decided to make himself a coffee and went into the adjoining kitchen area. He had only been in there a few minutes when he heard footsteps and the office door opening. He then heard a voice talking to someone on the telephone. He kept quiet and listened by the doorway.

'It's Hywel, have you got the goods? So when will you get them and when can I expect delivery, I need these urgently. Well, that's simply not good enough, I've got people here waiting for this lot. I wouldn't have entered into this arrangement with you if I'd realised you were going to mess me about.'

There was a long pause as whoever Hywel was talking to on the other end of the phone was explaining the situation to him.

'Well make sure it's next weekend then, you won't be getting any money from me until I get the goods, yes I'll have the cash, I'll be waiting.'

Just then the kettle boiled and alerted Hywel that he wasn't alone, he quickly ended the phone call and John Hughes, having made his coffee, decided to re-enter the office area.

'Good morning Hywel, it's not a bad morning,' said John as he continued to whistle as he came round the corner with a mug of coffee. 'The kettle's just boiled if you fancy a brew.'

'Morn... morning,' came the short-stuttered reply, 'how long have you been round there?'

'Oh, only a couple of minutes, I was just making the first brew of the day. Now then where was I?' said John, pretending to ignore the phone conversation and returning to the pile of paperwork as if he hadn't heard any of the conversation.

***

'Well this is going to keep me occupied for the next few days, sarge, the Lion has been busy over the weekend,' said Jean Price, as she highlighted the prisoner names in the report that she'd just opened that had been sent down from North Wales.

'Great, I can see he's been busy, I notice he hasn't as such made any inferences yet because you can bet your bottom dollar the DCI is going to be asking me for an update at the morning meeting.'

'No, it's a bit early for that yet, but I would think we might get something possibly by the end of the week. At this stage we still don't know what it is we are actually looking for. I mean there seems to be rival gang fighting going on in there and possibly early warning signs of a riot or two.'

***

Tim Ridgway made his way on his own into the dining hall for breakfast, he had a task this morning that he was not looking forward to one bit but nevertheless for his escape plan to work effectively he needed to do it.

Charlie had been up early and he was busy helping in the kitchen area. Tim took his tray of food and sat down on the same table where Higson was sitting with his mates.

'Morning Posh Boy, decided to come and sit with the big boys then?' said Higson, who was somewhat shocked that Tim had actually chosen to sit with him.

'Good morning Higson, I've been thinking about something you said last week,' hesitated Tim.

'Oh, yes, nice to know you have been thinking about me, and what would that be, I can always get you stuff, you know that.'

'I need a mobile phone and some wire cutters.'

'Keep your voice down, Posh Boy, else the screws will hear you.'

'Well, can you help me or not?'

'And what exactly do I get in return?'

'Well, you wanted some help with computer skills, didn't you?'

'Oh right, now look this is not the time or the place, let's discuss it later in association, in the meantime get on with your breakfast, Posh Boy.'

They continued eating their breakfast and for once Higson allowed Tim to eat his without any interference.

***

DCI Bentley had called DS Holdsworth and Jean Price, the crime analyst, over for an Operation Griffin review meeting in his office in Force HQ.

'So, DS Holdsworth, what exactly do we have so far on this operation? I understand our man has been over at the prison now for over a week so we should by now be at least picking up some inkling of the activity that is going on in there. I assume he's settled in and happy with the situation?'

'Well sir, I don't know whether he's happy with the situation but we have had our first report and whilst we have charted the prisoners of interest we haven't as yet uncovered any hint of what is being planned there. It is possible that we are looking at some sort of riot there but that is purely guesswork at present. All the incident activity in the prison seems to relate to the usual types of incident they get there, i.e. there is nothing out of the ordinary. I think we need to wait for a further update from the prison which we will probably get on Friday,' replied DS Holdsworth, who was frantically leafing through his notes.

'This doesn't make sense, Detective Sergeant, I mean our informant led us to believe there are external contacts involved here, they may well be planning a riot but I don't think that's what their end game is here. The riot could be a diversion to something far bigger.'

'Well I agree sir, but we don't yet have the full picture, it's all hypothetical at present.'

'Can I just interrupt and ask something, sir?' said Jean who was sitting listening patiently.

'Yes, of course Jean, please chip in,' said the DCI, who had almost seemed to have forgotten she was there.

'Well, whilst I realise we can't have the name of the informant who I gather has now been released from prison, can we at least have the details of which wing he was actually in. As I understand it HMP Dinas Bay operates where prisoners in one wing don't mix with other wings, unless they get transferred of course or moved for one reason or another. At least this way we can at least focus on the wing his information actually came from.'

'Good point Jean, I still think we need to have an overall view of what is going on in each wing because whatever they are planning could be prison wide but yes, the information he gave us must have primarily come from one specific wing. I'll find out from our informants section and get back to you. You can then pass that information back to our man in the prison. Well I have to say there is not much more we can achieve at present, let's meet up again, say next Monday at the same time. Thank you both for coming over.'

***

The bell rang for Association and Tim and Charlie made their way from their cell to the large community room in 'A' Wing. Tim hadn't mentioned his earlier conversation with Higson and Charlie was gobsmacked when Tim suddenly made his way over to speak to Higson.

'Is it a good time to talk now?' questioned Tim, who was still somewhat fearful of him.

'Might be, Posh Boy, let's go over to this corner.'

Charlie watched as Tim and Higson made their way over to a corner just next to the pool table, Higson's gang creating some form of cover from the watching eyes of the prison officers.

'So, you want a mobile then, is that with or without a SIM card?'

'Without, I will have my own SIM card, it needs to be a quality one right, no crap, a smartphone, a slim line one, not something like a brick from the 1990s, preferably an Android one.'

'Higson wouldn't know an Android one even if it got up and bit him on the arse,' chuckled one of Higson's mates.

'Course I would, shut up Brown and leave this to me, just stay out of it,' replied Higson in anger. 'Anyway, smuggling in one of those brick-like mobiles from the 90s would bring tears to your eyes. So right Posh Boy, how do you plan to charge this phone, I suppose you want me to get you a charger as well, that will be extra of course?'

'No, I don't need a charger.'

'What, so are you going to use bleeding magic to charge it then, Posh Boy?' said Higson, turning round as he fell about laughing with his mates.

'No, I've already thought of that, just get me the phone and the wire cutters.'

'So what exactly do you plan to use these for, Posh Boy?'

'That's none of your concern Higson, well can you get me them or not?' said Tim, getting impatient.

'I told you, Posh Boy, I can get you anything you like but as I say it will cost you and you have a skill we can use.'

'I realise that, so what do you want doing as payment in return?'

'Well, there is a CCTV camera located in the corner of the gymnasium, can you freeze it? I mean freeze it on demand from, say a mobile phone.'

Tim thought for a moment, you could almost hear the silence as he worked out how he could possibly achieve it.

'Yes, that shouldn't be a problem, so when do you want this?'

'You can!' said Higson, who couldn't believe his ears.

'So when exactly do you need this?' repeated Tim Ridgway, somewhat impatiently.

'As soon as possible, preferably before Christmas, do we have a deal?'

'Yes, we have a deal but why would you want to freeze the camera?'

'That's none of your business, Posh Boy,' said Higson tapping his nose, 'well can you do it or not?'

'Yes, but I must have the mobile phone and the cutters before I tackle that.'

'Good, I'll get it all organised straight away, in the meantime your cell mate Charlie is waiting for you so I suggest you get back to him. He'll be missing you by now,' said Higson sarcastically.

***

'Can we put the Christmas decorations up now mum?' said Emily excitedly.

'No, it's far too early Emily, it's not even December yet,' said Sue, who was busy making the children's tea.

'But the neighbours have got all their decorations up, inside and outside. Lucy has got her decorations up with even a tree lit up on their front lawn and a large Santa Claus on the chimney, why can't we, our house looks bare compared to hers, oh please can we mum, please?'

'No, I don't care what Lucy has got, look it won't be long Emily, let's wait at least until it's December.'

'I can't wait for Dad to come home Mum, is he really coming home for Christmas, it will be the bestest Christmas present ever?' said Tom enthusiastically.

'Yes, I'm sure he'll be back for Christmas Tom, I told you he rang me on Saturday, he said he's definitely going to be with us,' said Sue, who deep down would only believe it when he finally turned up.

***

He chose the brown leather one from the book shelf, sat down and carefully unpicked part of the stitching on the spine of the leather bible just enough to give him space to slot in two small hacksaw blades, two thin wires and a micro SIM card. Using the same thread he then re-stitched it and replaced it on the shelf.

CHAPTER 13

Wednesday 25th November, 2015

Tim Ridgway was busy on his rounds collecting laundry bags from 'A' wing ready for washing, he eventually arrived at Higson's cell.

'Now take good care of those, I don't want you to lose my socks like last time,' said Higson, as he winked at Tim and passed him out the laundry bag.

Tim was puzzled at first by the comment and thought surely he hasn't managed to get me the mobile phone and cutters already, he can't have in under two days, perhaps he's just being friendly or maybe he has a stock of them hidden away somewhere.

'Don't worry Higson, your laundry will be well looked after, I shall personally see to it myself,' replied Tim as he loaded the bag onto the trolley. He made a mental note of Higson's cell number and continued piling on the other bags from the other prisoners. He now made his way across to the Laundry room via the central spur, which was situated immediately across from the 'A' wing, and waited for the prison officer to allow him through. Once in the Laundry room he had to load six bags at a time into the industrial washing machines, he would then apply the washing powder and start the processing cycle. He made sure beforehand to watch out for Higson's cell numbered bag and when no one was looking he opened the bag, there at the top of Higson's washing pile was a pair of socks, one of which contained a mobile phone and the other the wire cutters. Tim swiftly pocketed them, re-tied the bag and loaded it into the machine with the other bags.

At the end of the day it was time to bring the laundry bags back to their individual owners so Tim and his two colleagues revisited the wing and distributed them accordingly.

Higson was waiting patiently in his cell for him.

'Have you managed to return my socks in one piece then, Posh Boy?'

'Yes, Higson, I think you'll find they are in two pieces actually, you'll find everything as you expected.'

'Smart arse,' sneered Higson as he took the laundry bag.

Tim now needed to hide the phone and wire cutters as quickly as possible. He returned to his cell, exhausted after his day's work, and when no one was looking unscrewed the u-bend under the small stainless steel sink in the cell. He firstly pushed the wire cutters inside the mattress of his bed and then wrapped the phone carefully inside two plastic bags he'd been keeping for the purpose and inserted it in the pipework. He'd just finished screwing the u-bend back when Charlie appeared from his daily duties in the kitchen.

'Hi Tim, what are you doing down there?'

'Oh, nothing Charlie, the water wasn't draining as fast as it should, I think I've fixed it now, just a lump of soap in there.'

'I hadn't realised you included plumbing as one of your skills, Tim.'

***

John Hughes once again had the security office to himself. Bill was off sick, Ian was on leave and Hywel had been assigned to the front security desk. It was just as John liked it, peaceful without the interruptions of Bill wanting to chat about anything other than work.

John picked up the pile of intelligence reports from the previous day and he was going through them carefully to classify and categorise each one before recording them onto the prison database. There were the usual types of incident such as drugs being found in a prisoner's cell and threats made to officers but he couldn't help noticing that there was one relating to Helen Morris, who had only just been seconded to work on 'A' wing temporarily. An officer on the wing had reported that two prisoners, Jason Williams and Owen

Montgomery, in particular had shown a keen interest in her and she had been shocked by their approach to her. It's maybe something or nothing he thought, as she was a very attractive woman but the officer felt he had to report it. John thought no more of it and entered it in the database; it was important that something that might seem innocent and not worth bothering with today could be important at a later date.

Six hours later he was on top of the job, he'd cleared the backlog and the database was right up to date. He sat back in his chair with his hands folded behind his head and considered the types of report that he should process which would help him in producing his weekly surveillance report ready for transmission back to Midshire Police. It was an ideal time, the office was quiet, he could perform his research, produce his reports without being spotted but he'd forgotten one vital aspect to all this, the audit log.

***

Helen Morris was now working shifts in the prison. She'd been seconded from Security to Operations for an unspecified period and she was now assigned to 'B' wing. Her first day had been a bit of a nightmare with prisoners banging on doors and wolf whistling whenever she came into the wing area. She was assured this would calm down once the inmates had got used to her. Her secondment however did have its useful side as she could advise the officers on the importance of completing intelligence reports correctly, an added bonus from a security point of view.

She was on the afternoon shift today and had taken a break to grab something to eat in the staff canteen when a fellow officer came in and sat down beside her.

'You are new here, aren't you?' said the officer.

'Well, I'm not new to the prison but yes I've been seconded from the Security Department, not sure for how long. I'll be here on shifts and I'm not good at getting up early. It'll be a bit of a struggle for me on mornings,' replied Helen.

'Yes, they take some getting used to, I'm new here myself actually having transferred from HMP Bude Hall down in Devon. Before that I was in Exeter House which was an experience I can tell you, certainly nothing like these modern prisons. We enjoyed living in Devon, lovely county, still it's a lovely part of the country here and the family and I feel really settled now in North Wales.'

'Did you say you were in Exeter House? A colleague of mine in security here has just transferred from there.'

'Really, who is that?'

'John Hughes, he was a security officer there,' replied Helen.

'Bloody hell, John Hughes, yes I remember him a tall guy with a beard, likes the sound of his own voice.'

'Yes, that's right, he has only been with us a week or so.'

'Well fancy that. Who'd have thought it, I remember John Hughes, a right boring bastard, shit he could bore for England, sorry I hope he's not a friend of yours.'

'No, but to be quite honest he didn't strike me as boring, but as I say I've only known him about a week.'

CHAPTER 14

Saturday 28th November, 2015

Tim Ridgway sat waiting patiently in his cell. Today he was expecting a visitor who would provide a most important piece of his escape plan jigsaw. Saturday could be a most boring day in prison with inmates having no work as such to take their mind off everything, particularly if a prisoner had no visitors that day to look forward to. Prisoners would sit around waiting for visitors, sit in their cells reading, watching TV or visiting the gymnasium. In Charlie's case he still had no visitors or any likelihood of any coming and Tim did all he could to cheer him up.

'So who have you got coming in today then, Tim?'

'It's Father O'Brien who is popping in to see me, I don't think he'll be stopping for long,' replied Tim who at this stage didn't wish to tell Charlie of his plans just yet.

'Father O'Brien again!' he exclaimed. 'Are you turning to religion all of a sudden, Tim? This is getting serious, isn't it?'

'Well to be honest Charlie, yes I am feeling slightly more religious these days and I'm hoping God will forgive me for all the trouble and despair that I've piled on people. I really bitterly regret what I've done and when I eventually get out of this place I'm determined to go straight.'

***

John Hughes decided to travel into Caernarvon on the Saturday morning to stock up on provisions for the weeks ahead. He parked up in Doc Fictoria set alongside the beautiful harbour which looked out across the scenic Menai Straits. He made his way into the historic town centre. Shopping was not really his thing but he enjoyed the pre-Christmas bustle and activity within the town centre. The skies were already grey and threatening and the weather forecast was not good for the weekend. He'd decided to get everything done before Storm Clodagh arrived, which was originally expected on the Sunday morning, leaving him free to type up his report.

After stocking up with food and drink he made his way back to the caravan park. The rain was already lashing down as he drove down the narrow country lanes. By now the sky was almost black and the wind was howling in the trees. He stepped into the caravan, switched on the lighting even though it was mid-day and suddenly the noise on the roof was deafening as the monsoon rain and hail beat down incessantly. He poured himself a beer and thought about creating his weekly report.

He logged into his laptop first, just to see if he had any messages from HQ, and to his surprise there were two messages, one from DS Holdsworth requesting him to attend an online web meeting on Monday 30th November at 10.00am and the other from Jean Price asking him to specifically focus on 'A' wing.

***

The prison visitor waiting room was packed and somewhat noisy with crying children running around in the visitor centre and it was standing room only. With severe gale force storms being forecast for the whole weekend most visitors had travelled earlier than normal to make sure they had arrived in plenty of time. Eventually a prison officer came and opened the doors ready for the security screening process prior to entering the visitor meeting area.

'Ah, good afternoon Father, it's good to see you again, please sign in, I remember you set the alarm off last time when you arrived so we'll dispense with that aspect. If you would like to go straight through, you are on, let me see, yes table 23 on the right hand side.'

He made his way through to table 23 and Tim arrived moments later.

'Good afternoon Father, it's good to see you again and thanks for coming over.'

'Good afternoon Tim, I remembered you asked for a bible so here it is, I know you will get a lot of pleasure and comfort from this.'

'I will indeed Father and thank you ever so much,' replied Tim, taking hold of the bible and leafing through the pages.

After discussion about conditions in the prison, forgiveness, life in general and news on the outside it was time to go.

'Well thank you once again, Father, I really appreciate you coming over.'

'Thank you Tim, just call me if you need me, you know where I am, goodbye for now.'

CHAPTER 15

Monday 30th November, 2015

Most of the UK had received a battering over the weekend from Storm Clodagh with gusts in excess of 60 miles per hour. The gale force winds and high tides from the Irish Sea pounded the Welsh coastline, damaging the sea defences and wreaking havoc across the entire country. Flights and ferry services were cancelled, trains delayed and the entire transport network at times grinded to a halt. On Sunday the fierce winds rocked John Hughes's caravan so much throughout the day and night that he had no sleep whatsoever. When morning came the winds had subsided a little but John had already decided he needed to ring in sick in order that he could attend the online web meeting with Force HQ. He called the main switchboard at the prison and told them that he may be in later that day if he was feeling well enough. He'd already transferred his report to HQ on the Sunday morning in readiness for the meeting.

John Hughes connected his laptop and satisfied the security login, everyone else was online in readiness and up on the screen came the camera view of the DCI's office.

'Good morning, I think we have everyone here now, right I'll start by summarising how I see it,' said the DCI, opening up the debate. 'It is quite clear that at this stage we still don't have a handle on what it is that we think is being planned in the prison. We have a list of possible suspects who may be connected with this but again it is guesswork on our part. The chief constable is becoming somewhat impatient as he thought by now we would have at least an inkling of what we could expect. If we are not careful we could very well find ourselves on the back foot chasing the problem when it has already happened. Is this a fair assumption, DS Holdsworth?'

'Yes, sir, I'm afraid that does seem to be the situation but to be fair we have only been in the prison for two weeks and these things do take time.'

'Yes, I appreciate that DS Holdsworth, but I'm not sure we have time on our side. Now we have the latest surveillance report from DC Hodgson which arrived over the weekend. Now then Jack, or should I call you John, you're the man on the inside, we've read your reports to date but how do you see it at the moment?'

Just at that moment, when John Hughes was about to speak, there came a noisy tapping on the caravan bedroom window. John opened the curtains and there was Edward Jones, the caravan site owner.

'Good morning, is everything alright Mr Hughes?' shouted Edward Jones, 'we were worried about you and wondered if you had suffered any damage in the storms or were suffering from any illness?'

'Yes, everything is fine Mr Jones, I'll give you a call later, I'm on the phone at present,' said John Hughes, closing the curtains and returning to the computer screen.

'Sorry about that everyone, a bit of an unexpected interruption I'm afraid. Well sir, as I see it there are a number of suspects worth looking at in closer detail. These are referred to in my summary page on my last report. Firstly Arthur Higson – he's been in and out of prison ever since he left school, he is on the category of Bullying, he is serving a sentence of eight years at present for armed robbery. He seems to be the leader of a gang on 'A' wing and is suspected of bringing drugs into the prison. Officers on his wing have searched his cell multiple times and never found anything. Higson frequently appears on the intelligence reports each week. Secondly we have a prisoner by the name of John Fowler, he by all accounts is a nasty piece of work who seems to be running a business from inside, again we don't know what exactly he is up to but he is on a watch list. He is serving a sentence of ten years and is in for various fraud offences. Another name I am interested in is Derek Arrowsmith, he is in 'A' wing and has been found with a substantial quantity of drugs inside his mattress. He is also connected with Higson. One of the names that has also come to my attention is that of Tariq

Atiq, originally from our force area, who is on 'D' wing. It is early days but I think Tariq could be being groomed for terrorism, he has been showing signs that once he is out he will pursue some kind of terrorist attack. He is one we are watching carefully. Now we come onto someone who is not actually a prisoner but an officer, he could well be the external link in all this lot. His name is Hywel Jones and he works in Prison Security of all places. Unlikely as it seems that a security officer is involved you will see from my report that I overheard him on the telephone discussing receiving "stuff" and becoming somewhat irate with whoever he was talking to. I think we need to know more on Mr Hywel Jones so you will see that I am suggesting we obtain call records, bank transactions, etc. to see exactly what he is up to. I appreciate you will need to get authority to do that. Finally we come to Timothy John Ridgway, who you may remember from our bank card and identity theft investigations a few months ago. He is also on 'A' wing and could possibly be involved. A recent intelligence report connects him with Higson although I have some doubts that he is involved. So there we have it sir, sorry I cannot be more specific.'

'Thank you DC Hodgson, most interesting but tell me why you think Ridgway is not involved, or more to the point why you have doubts about him,' replied the DCI, who had been scribbling notes down throughout.

'Well sir, Ridgway had only arrived here just before me on the 2nd of November and would not have been in the prison when our informant was here.'

'Yes, I appreciate that, but that doesn't say that he hasn't been roped into it now, after all as you say he has connections with Higson who seems to be the gang leader in there.'

'I suggest we follow up Hywel Jones, sir, I think he is worth following up.'

'Are you quite serious, DC Hodgson?'

'Yes sir, there is something not quite right with Hywel Jones, I can't put my finger on it but I think we need to investigate him. It's only a hunch but I think he could be involved in bringing in drugs.'

'Very well, let's follow up Mr Hywel Jones and see where that takes us. Jean, can you complete the appropriate paperwork to obtain his call records, bank statements, etc. and I will go upstairs and get it approved.'

'Very good sir, will do,' replied Jean, who had been making notes directly into her laptop.

'DC Hodgson, can you find out what you can about Hywel Jones ready for our next meeting, there may be clues into what he is doing in his spare time which could help us here.'

'Will do, sir.'

'Well that will be all for now everyone, thank you for your time, a useful meeting, let's hope we are going down the right path. Can I suggest we meet again say a week today, shall we say the same time? We'll let DC Hodgson get back to his day job.'

'If possible sir, can I suggest we hold the meeting at six pm, otherwise I'll have to get time off work,' replied John Hughes.

'Yes, sorry I should have thought about that. Six o'clock next Monday evening.'

John Hughes closed down the secure web session, switched off the laptop and started to prepare to go into work. As he got changed into his prison uniform he couldn't help thinking back to the sudden interruption by Edward Jones and how did he know about his illness that he hadn't actually got.

**

Jean Price returned to her desk and researched Hywel Jones's personal data to obtain the necessary details. He had been with the prison service a number of years and was now married with four children. His wife worked in the local primary school as a classroom assistant and they were in the process of buying their own house about five miles from the prison. He had two mobile phones as far as she could make out. She then completed the appropriate paperwork to obtain the call records for both phones belonging to him and passed it to DCI Bentley for approval. It was then passed back and issued to the SPOC unit (Single Point of Contact) to obtain the details from the service provider.

She had started now to build up quite a database of connections but there was still no clear picture emerging of what it was that was being planned. Hopefully they would soon have the call records coming in so she could at least download those and analyse any connections found.

***

John Hughes arrived in work at lunchtime and was greeted by Bill Gardner, who was busy in the office.

'Glad you could make it, John, I could see the pile of intelligence reports building up here particularly if you were going to be off for a while. I assume you are feeling much better now?'

'Yes, thanks Bill, just a bit of a stomach upset, I don't think it's anything serious or catching for that matter.'

'Good, it sounds like the results of a jolly good weekend to me.'

'Well I must admit I did have one or two beers too many on the Saturday night down at the Smithy Arms and, coupled with a lack of sleep from the weekend storms, I didn't feel too good afterwards. It's normally pretty peaceful in the caravan, I've had some of the best sleeps I've ever had in there.'

'So how is the house hunting going, surely you can't be planning to spend the whole winter in the caravan, it must be pretty damn cold in there?'

'Well the house hunting is on hold at present until we sell our own,' said John Hughes, lying through his teeth, 'and to be honest it's not that cold, in fact it's quite cosy, you'd be surprised.'

'Well at least you should be able to get home for Christmas, some of us here have got to work through it, you are one of the lucky ones at least spending it with the family.'

'Yes, I'll be glad to get home and see them all over Christmas, I'll be thinking of you working in here when I'm carving the roast turkey,' teased John Hughes.

'Yes, I'm sure you will,' laughed Bill. 'I can't complain, I've had the last two Christmases on leave.'

'It's a bit quiet in here again Bill, there are a few missing, where are they?' said John, looking around the office.

'Yes, they are falling like flies John, Ian has also rung in sick and Hywel had already booked a day off for a pre-Christmas visit to see his mother in Dun Laoghaire. With Helen on secondment to Operations I'm pleased you have at least managed to make it in.'

John immediately thought that's interesting, with no flights and the Irish ferries cancelled through the bad weather so why would Hywel continue with having a day off. He put the thought to one side and logged in and read the weekend summary review from Operations. There was nothing of any real interest, Higson had been in trouble again, this time fighting in the exercise yard but apart from that no real dramas to speak of. He then continued to read in detail the actual intelligence reports and started to update the system.

**

Tim had decided at some point very soon he needed to take Charlie into his confidence and outline to him his escape plan. He was trying to delay the moment as long as he possibly could, he now had everything he needed although first he had to complete his part of the bargain with Higson. He'd decided that as soon as he had finished his laundry rounds he would need to prepare for a night of research and coding but before he could do that he would first need to charge up the mobile phone and he could only do that in the middle of the night. Yes the time had definitely come, he had no option but to let Charlie know of his plans and hope he would buy into them. He waited for his moment, which came when they were walking in the exercise yard later that afternoon.

'Charlie, you know I'm determined to get out of here.'

'Yes, I realise that Tim, you've been on about nothing else since the day you arrived but this place is like Fort Knox, you've got no chance without being caught. I mean this place has been purpose-built, no one has ever escaped from here.'

'Well I think you're wrong Charlie, we can get out of here, I've worked it out.'

'What do you mean, we, are you assuming that I'll be going with you?'

'Yes, it is a we, I have a plan that both of us can get out of here but it does need the both of us.'

'Oh, I don't know about this Tim, if we get caught it will be an even longer stretch in prison. In any case in a strange sort of way I feel I'd be better off in here at present, my family don't want to know me, I have no home anymore, at least here I get three meals a day, a bed, tv and no hassle from the outside world.'

Tim was staggered that Charlie was thinking this way and he was starting to have second thoughts about taking him into his confidence but whilst he shared a cell with him he really had no choice in the matter.

'Look we need to have a long chat, I'm getting out of here, I will outline my plan to you but it does need you to be a part of it,' said Tim, who was now having serious doubts whether Charlie would even get involved in his masterplan.

As Charlie was protesting to Tim the hooter went and it was time for them to return to the wing.

CHAPTER 16

Tuesday 1st December, 2015

Tim Ridgway had been up early, very early in fact, he needed to charge the mobile phone that Higson had provided him with. He switched the small bedside light on and went over to the sink. As quietly as he could he removed the mobile phone from under the sink and crept back into bed. He then carefully unpicked the stitching on the leather bible and removed the two wires and the SIM card. He inserted the SIM card into the phone and then re-stitched the bible. As quietly as he could he then started to dismantle his electric shaving razor that Alan from the Jelly Bean had sent him.

He attached the wires to the shaver and connected the other ends to the mobile phone battery connectors using chewing gum to hold them in place. He plugged the shaver in, switched his light off and retired back to bed. By the time Charlie had woken up in the morning the phone was charged and back in its hiding place.

***

'Good morning Hywel, did you enjoy your day off?' asked John Hughes, as he hung his anorak on the coat rack.

'Yes, thanks,' came the short grunt of a reply.

Hywel was busy reading, not the incident reports which he should have been doing, but the sports pages of the local daily newspaper.

'Did you get caught out in the weekend storms, Hywel?'

'No, it didn't bother me.'

'I don't suppose you've organised a username and password for me yet?'

'No.'

John decided that talking to Hywel was like trying to get blood out of a stone and that he wouldn't bother wasting any more time in any more meaningless conversation and sat down. He logged in once again using Hywel's details and pressed on with his workload. He was deeply engrossed in a couple of intelligence reports from 'B' wing when the Head of Security Tom Fletcher came in, accompanied by Bill Gardner and Ian Roberts.

'Good morning chaps,' shouted Tom Fletcher, 'can I just have your attention, the governor has requested that we all meet in five minutes time in his office, a situation has arisen that we need an urgent meeting, and before you ask I don't have any further details on this.'

John Hughes hadn't yet met the governor, he'd seen him from a distance when Bill Gardner had pointed him out in the staff canteen but he had that pleasure to come. The four men made their way up the stairs to the top corridor where the governor's suite of offices was located. They entered the room marked 'Gold Command Room' and took their seats around the large meeting room table. Minutes later a tall, silver-haired gentleman in a smart navy-blue suit arrived. He was assisted by his PA Jane Shone who took a seat beside him and handed him a document from the folder she was carrying.

'Good morning gentlemen, thank you for coming up at such short notice, I realise you have busy workloads and I promise that I will not keep you here too long.'

Just then the governor noticed John Hughes and nodded over to him.

'Good morning, I don't believe we have met, I'm Richard Smethurst, I gather you have joined us from HMP Exeter House. You must be John Hughes, welcome onboard, Tom Fletcher has told me all about you.'

'Good morning sir, it's good to meet you,' responded John Hughes, who didn't really expect any special treatment and thought hopefully he doesn't know all about me.

'Well gentlemen, I realise your department manages the intelligence system and you are in effect providing us with early warnings of problems and issues affecting the prison, however there is a potential situation which has come to our notice through an anonymous letter, sent from outside directly to me, which you won't be aware of. Naturally I will give you a copy of this letter after the meeting. We don't know whether this is a letter from a member of staff or a prisoner's family but it states a number of concerns with regard to inadequate staffing and increasing unrest within the prison. It goes on to say that stress is starting to show and if something is not done about it there are rumours that the inmates are planning to start a riot. It states that you will have noticed that a number of prison officers have also recently resigned and are not prepared to continue with the existing situation. I dispute this of course as I don't think it's quite as bad as the letter makes out but nevertheless we need to take action to prevent such a riot. Firstly can I ask any of you whether any of the recent intelligence reports reflect this?'

'Well sir, as far as I can see this could be just a seasonal issue; with Christmas on the horizon certain inmates are clearly unhappy about being locked up away from their families and as you know under the new government scheme some prisoners are being released early. This too could have an effect,' replied Tom Fletcher.

'Well, we have seen a number of intelligence reports in the past week indicating there may be problems ahead but nothing as such to take any real action just yet,' replied John Hughes, who carefully chose his words and didn't wish to rock Tom Fletcher's boat.

'I think sir that the problem may be related only to certain wings, the reports that John is referring to are in fact confined to 'B' wing,' said Bill Gardner.

Hywel and Ian remained silent and just nodded in the appropriate places.

'So gentlemen I am proposing that we keep a careful eye on this for the time being, but if the situation changes we may well have to review the Christmas period staffing levels. Thank you all for coming and now I'll let you get back to the job in hand. Tom, here is a copy of the letter for your records.'

'Thank you sir, we will add this to the intel database.'

With that the governor and his PA left the room.

As soon as the door had closed Tom was the first to speak.

'Well that will go down like a lead balloon, if we have to increase the staffing level over Christmas there will be hell to pay, a lot of our staff have already made arrangements for time off.'

'Me included,' said John despondently.

***

After a morning's hard work in the Laundry Tim Ridgway made his way into the dining hall, he was starving with hunger after what had been a busy morning. He grabbed a tray, got in the queue and eventually he was served by Charlie Ellis, his cell mate.

'Hi Tim, you look a bit knackered, have you had a busy one?'

'You can say that again, we are a man down at present, Wilkinson has gone sick and has been transferred to the Medical Centre, I think he's putting it on a bit. To be honest I could do with a good sleep but I'm not going to get it,' said Tim, yawning. 'I really need to get over to the gymnasium as soon as I've finished today.'

'Good God, that's a bit drastic, are you sure you can find the place, I don't think you've even been over there since you've arrived, you take it easy, don't go overdoing it.'

'No, I thought I'd have half an hour and try and get some exercise in,' said Tim, who was now being interrupted by inmates behind him telling him to get a bloody move on.

'I'll see you later, Charlie.'

Tim found a quiet corner and ate his meal in peace, he had a number of things on his mind but for now the priority was to identify the details of the CCTV camera in the gymnasium.

***

'It's December now mummy, you said we can put up the Christmas decorations,' shouted Emily excitedly as she entered the kitchen.

'Are you not dressed for school yet young lady, now come on and get a move on or else we'll be late,' replied Sue who was hastily making the children's breakfast.

'But can we mummy? Please, you did say we could.'

'Yes of course, look we'll all put them up together later on after you both come home from school, now come on back up those stairs quick and get changed.'

'Mum have you seen my shorts, I've got PE later on today and I can't find them anywhere,' shouted Tom from the top of the stairs.

'No, I haven't, where did you last leave them?'

'I can't remember, I may have left them in school last week.'

'Well, that's probably where you'll find them, how do you expect me to know that. Now come on and get a move on or I'll be late for work. The sooner your father returns home the better,' said Sue, who clearly had her hands full looking after the children on her own.

***

Tim had finished his work and although he was tired and exhausted he made his way down to the gymnasium. It was relatively quiet and he took his place on the cross trainer. He didn't want to make it obvious that he was purely there on reconnaissance so continued for about five minutes. Looking around he could see there was just one CCTV camera positioned in the far corner, presumably it was set to give a wide view of the room. He then moved across to a row of exercise bikes placed just in front of the camera. He pedalled away for a few minutes and looked up and could see an asset number which had been typed onto a label on the underside of the camera. He made a mental note of the five digit number and decided he'd had enough exercise for the day. Ten minutes later he was back in his cell.

CHAPTER 17

Friday 4th December, 2015

'Good morning Jean, I think these are what you are waiting for,' said DS Holdsworth as he handed over a hard copy of Hywel Jones's telephone call records to Jean Price. 'How long will you need to analyse these?'

'I'll need a few days, sarge, and ideally I would have preferred them in electronic form but no matter I can soon scan them in.'

'I think the boss was hoping we might have something for our meeting on Monday evening but it is as it is.'

'Well leave it with me, I'll see what I can come up with for Monday's meeting, I might have to work through the weekend though, sarge.'

'Well no problem there Jean, if you need extra hours then that's fine by me, put in whatever hours you need.'

***

John Hughes was glad to see the end of the week, he'd been working flat out trying to keep pace with the increasing workload in the Security Department. Hywel had been temporarily assigned to 'C' wing which pleased John as he was the most miserable colleague to work with. The governor was now showing considerably more interest in the potential riot situation and requesting a number of ad hoc reports from the database which John had to produce. At one point the governor even considered bringing in the police but of course it was still early days and pure rumour at this stage and based on the evidence to date he wouldn't have got the necessary support. John decided after pulling together all the data he needed for his weekly report back to Midshire to call it a day and he drove back to the caravan park. He parked up and decided to have an early shower, a quick change and headed down to the Smithy Arms for something to eat.

The olde worlde pub looked absolutely delightful fully decked out, inside and out with Christmas decorations, everywhere was lit up but it was quiet again. This was the first time John felt really homesick and wished he could be back with his wife and family.

'Someone's been busy, the place looks fantastic,' said John as he entered the lounge bar.

'I've been at this lot all day, quite a job I can tell you, so what will you be having then?' replied Steve the landlord.

John ordered himself a pint of best bitter and the pie of the day. He sat down in the corner by the stone and slate inglenook fireplace. He'd decided to forget all about the data and his report for the time being, all he wanted to do now was sit back and relax. He had just sat down alongside the roaring log fire and opened the newspaper but who should come in but Bill Gardner.

'I thought I'd find you here John, I've been over to the caravan but there was no one there apart from some old bloke wandering around wanting to know the ins and outs of the cat's arse so to speak.'

'Hi Bill, that would be Edward by the way, the campsite owner. Anyway I didn't know you lived around here?'

'I don't but Tom Fletcher asked me to try and contact you and I don't have your mobile number, we are short of staff on Sunday on the wings and the governor is desperate to make sure we have the right manpower levels to avoid any problems. Is there any chance you can make it in? It's a twelve hour shift on days I'm afraid.'

'Well I can do without it,' said John, 'but I'm not doing anything as it happens, yes ok, count me in, I'll be there.'

'Great, I'll tell Tom, he'll appreciate it, well I'll leave you to it, see you on Sunday morning eight o'clock.'

'Are you not stopping for a quick one?'

'No, I must get off, tempting as it is, the wife will have my dinner ready, see you Sunday,' replied Bill as he left the pub.

John Hughes thought well so much for a relaxing weekend and as soon as he had finished his meal he headed back to the caravan to work on his report. The caravan was bitterly cold when he got in but soon warmed up after he'd switched on the old gas fire. He switched on the TV to catch up on the local and national news; there was another strong weather warning with Storm Desmond due to hit Wales, the North West and Scotland with heavy rain and gales forecast. The rain had already started, steadily beating down on the caravan roof. He settled down to work on his laptop when suddenly there was a knock on the door. He peered through the window and opened it slightly to find Edward the campsite owner standing there.

'You've had a visitor Mr Hughes, I thought you ought to know, I found him snooping round the caravan, well knocking on the door to be more precise, shifty looking character if you bloody ask me.'

'Yes, thank you Mr Jones, I have seen him, he came over to the pub.'

'Yes, I told him you might be over there, if you see him again can you ask him to please observe the no speeding sign, it was like bloody Brands Hatch around here.'

'Yes thank you Mr Jones, I'm very busy at the moment but I'll tell him, goodbye for now,' replied John Hughes, closing the window.

John Hughes cracked on with his report and eventually when he fell asleep at the laptop he decided to call it a night, he'd spent all evening typing up the report which included details of the meeting he had recently had with the governor. He couldn't help thinking whether the planned activity related to a riot or was there something much more sinister behind all this, time will tell. The weather forecast for the weekend was not good and John settled down for the night.

***

Tim Ridgway had waited for Charlie to leave the cell and return to his kitchen duties in the late afternoon. After he'd gone he retrieved the mobile phone and then hid it under his mattress until nightfall when everywhere was on lock down and Charlie was fast asleep. He was surprised how good the signal was and he managed to download the two apps he was after in a very short time. He ran the first app and immediately started the sniffing process across the CCTV network. He'd made a note of the asset number of the camera in the gymnasium and waded through the list of cameras; after about two minutes there it was showing the IP address of the camera. He then ran his second app, typed in the IP address and was prompted for a password. He tried the obvious ones such as *0000, 1234* and the word *password* itself, all were rejected. He thought this is going to take longer than he first thought and then he hit on a brainwave, he typed in the five digit asset number and bingo he was connected, whoever had set up the network of over 200 CCTV cameras in the prison had been lazy and taken the easy way out and defaulted to the asset number for each one. He now knew that once he knew the asset number he could get access to every CCTV camera in the prison, and that bit was easy as they had printed it on the underneath of each one. He now had to make preparations to code the necessary software routine to freeze the CCTV camera for Higson. This wasn't going to be easy without access to a computer. He knew he couldn't do it all on the phone itself and needed help from outside to create the app initially on a PC. As he didn't have access to any computer in the prison he decided to contact one of his fellow students from his university days, James Whitmore, who was a whizz with mobile development. Tim put together as best he could a description on what it was he was after, told him it was urgent and emailed it to James.

Two hours later he received an email back from James saying he was straight onto it and would get back to him shortly.

***

Jean Price had decided to work the weekend if she was to have any chance of performing analysis on Hywel Jones's call records in readiness for Monday's meeting. The two mobile phones belonging to Hywel Jones were under two different service providers and subsequently the format of the call records that she'd received from the SPOC unit were different. This just made further work for Jean as she scanned the documents into her spreadsheet ready for importing into the Link Analysis database. By mid-afternoon on the Saturday she had imported the data and now it was time to see if there were any connections with the existing data. She powered up the software and explored the links on the two phones. Almost immediately she could see a cluster of calls which had been made very early in the morning. The calls however were to mobile numbers which were not on the database. One number in particular stood out a mile.

***

By now Storm Desmond had arrived and made its entrance in grand style, the fourth storm of the season and was already beginning to wreak havoc along the North Wales coast but it was nothing like the damage it did much further up the coast in Cumbria. The eighty mile an hour winds rocked the caravan and heavy rain lashed down on the roof. John Hughes had had a very disturbed night and the noise and shaking had kept him awake almost all night.

When he did finally wake on the Saturday morning he switched on the TV to catch the local news and the damage was there for all to see, fallen trees, flooding, blocked roads, collapsed bridges and roads, cancelled trains. He was lucky that the caravan hadn't turned over in the high winds. He wondered if he would be able to get a connection from his laptop to send in his report. He had a quick shower and set about connecting into the server to transmit his latest report. Surprisingly he managed to connect to the Midshire server first time and uploaded his report in readiness for the next meeting. He then opened the curtains and looking out of the front window was shocked with what he saw. One of the other static caravans across the way was now on its side and had been pushed over by a fallen oak tree. There was a gaping hole in the side which was exposed to the elements, water was pouring into the caravan. He looked up the emergency number that Edward Jones had left and he contacted him immediately to inform him of the damage. Minutes later from around the corner came Edward Jones in his old van followed by a trail of black smoke. John went out to meet him outside the wreck of the caravan.

'Good God Mr Hughes, I've never seen anything as bad as this, we've had storms before but nothing on this scale. This caravan belongs to Mrs Helmsley over in Stoke-on-Trent. She's been coming here for donkey's years. She'll be so upset when I tell her. I'll have to give her a call once I've arranged to have it removed to a safe place. It does look as though this is the only one damaged so I guess it could have been much worse.'

'Quite a storm, Mr Jones, hopefully the worst is over now. Do you need a hand with any of this?'

'No, thank you all the same Mr Hughes, one of my farming friends will come over and sort this out for me but I will need to take a few photographs before it gets removed. Thanks again for calling me, I'll be off now.'

CHAPTER 18

Sunday 6th December, 2015

John Hughes turned up at the prison earlier than normal, it was a day he wasn't really looking forward to. Up until this point his duties had meant he could reside in the Security office and keep off the wings. He was apprehensive that someone from his past might possibly recognise him, someone who he may have interviewed years ago who would be quick to blow his cover. He made his way into the Security Department where Bill Gardner was sitting waiting patiently.

'Glad you could make it John, you've been assigned to 'A' wing and I'm on 'B' wing. If you make your way down there the duty officer will go through everything with you. I'll see you back up here just before we go off shift.'

John made his way through the labyrinth of corridors, landings and locked doors and eventually arrived at the duty officer's desk on 'A' wing.

'Ah you must be the temp for the day,' said the officer. 'Welcome onboard John, my name is Greg Henderson, we shouldn't have too much trouble with these today. Most of them have visitors this afternoon and in two hours' time they will be in the chapel for the morning service.'

Greg Henderson was a beast of a man, muscular and weighing probably over twenty stone and close on seven feet. He clearly wouldn't take any nonsense from anyone. He was a relief prison officer and worked across the region's prisons.

'You say most of them, I hadn't realised they were so religious.'

'Well they are not to be honest but it gives them time to meet up and have a chat, presumably do a bit of business but I don't go there so best not to ask. I suggest you stick with me and you'll be fine.'

They made their way down the noisy corridor filled with every type of music blasting out of the different cells, reggae, rap, rock, heavy metal, you name it.

'Turn it down boys, I can't hear myself think,' shouted Greg into one or two of the noisier cells. 'They are not a bad bunch on this wing, a few troublemakers like Higson but generally they are easy to look after. Some of them will be released earlier than their sentence next week, a government initiative to free up some space. They'll be under strict licence of course and any problems they'll be straight back in here. Some of course can't survive out there, prison is all they know, they are like fish out of water. What concerns me though is the ones who are not going to be allowed out early, they could kick off at any moment if we are not careful.'

Just then shouting broke out in a nearby cell, it was clear some form of argument was taking place between cell mates in A105.

'That'll be Morrison and Reynolds, who even though they share a cell together don't always get on, you hang on here John, I'll just go in and calm the situation down,' said Greg Henderson, leaving John Hughes alone for a few minutes.

Almost immediately and what clearly seemed to be timed by the disturbance, Higson appeared out of his cell and approached John Hughes in the corridor.

'Higson's the name, you are new here, aren't you? Although your face is somewhat familiar, now where have I seen you before, it will come to me, just give me a minute, anyway how long have you been working here?'

'Quite new Higson, just a few weeks, I transferred from another prison. I'm pretty sure we haven't met before, why do you ask?' responded John Hughes, who had read all about Higson and for the first time was finally face to face with him.

'Well put it this way, do you want to make some easy money guv, just ready for Christmas, payment in cash of course, all strictly hypothetical of course,' Higson said in a whispered voice.

John Hughes was stunned. 'And what exactly would be my involvement in this so called easy money scheme then?' he said, keeping his voice down and just going along with it.

'Well, it's just supposing, hypothetically of course, you brought us something in from outside, we'd make it worth your while and if it goes well we could see about making it a bit more of a regular event. Maybe there could even be an added bonus in it for you. Call it a loyalty bonus.'

'Bit risky, you are asking for trouble,' replied John shaking his head.

'Life's full of risk guv, but we'd make it worth your while, this is all hypothetical of course.'

'Really, well leave it with me and I'll have to think about it.'

'Don't take too long guv and of course we haven't even had this conversation. In any case it's all hypothetical!'

'Of course I quite understand, leave it with me.'

Just then Greg Henderson reappeared from the cell having silenced the inmates.

'Is everything alright John? You seem to be in a bit of a state of shock.'

'Everything is fine Greg, just fine,' replied John, who was now already thinking of writing his own first intelligence report.

***

Tim Ridgway had no visitors planned for the Sunday afternoon so he'd decided he would stay in his cell and check to see if James had managed to develop the app. He didn't need anything fancy, just a basic app. When no one was looking he quickly logged into his emails on his mobile and sure enough there it was, the link for him to download the app that James had developed for him overnight. The prison was quieter than normal, inmates were either in the visiting centre, playing snooker, reading or just watching TV. As Charlie wasn't expecting any visitors he'd been asked to go to the kitchen to prepare for the evening meals. Tim now had the perfect opportunity to download and test the program. Two hours later he made his way to the gymnasium with the mobile in his pocket. There was no one in there and he had the place to himself. Tim had previously typed into the device the CCTV IP address for the gymnasium and entered the password, he found a quiet corner just outside the scope of the camera and pressed the freeze button on the App. At that point the image was frozen and the only way he could test it was by capturing the live screen and comparing it with what was being pushed out to the monitors up in the Security Department. He clearly knew he would be in big trouble if he was caught. He stepped into the view of the camera, turned his back to it and checked it on the mobile, yes, sure enough he couldn't be seen on the monitors. He

158

stepped back into the corner, selected freeze off returning the monitor image to the live view. He returned to his cell, a job well done, all he had to do now was copy the routine onto Higson's phone.

***

John Hughes returned to the caravan tired and exhausted after his twelve hour shift, he switched on the TV and was staggered at the damage the storms over the weekend had done, particularly in Cumbria. To his surprise he noticed that the damaged caravan had already been removed. All that remained was the hard standing and the pipework which had been sealed off. He had eaten in work in the staff canteen but felt a bit peckish and made himself a quick beans and toast. He couldn't help thinking back to the conversation he had had with Higson, he had lots of questions in his head, was this a one off or part of a much bigger problem, should he get involved to try and uncover what exactly they were up to, were other officers involved, was it a coincidence that Greg Henderson disappeared quickly into Morrison's cell at the time that Higson appeared. While he was pondering on this he dozed off in the chair before eventually waking up at midnight and retiring to his bed.

CHAPTER 19

Monday 7th December, 2015

'I need your phone for about thirty minutes,' said Tim Ridgway as he grabbed hold of Higson's arm in the canteen.

'You must be joking Posh Boy, you've got a bloody phone, don't tell me you put it in with the laundry and anyway keep your bloody voice down!' whispered Higson.

'No, of course not, look I've developed that app you need, do you want that job doing or not, I will need access to your phone if you want the ability to freeze a CCTV frame.'

'Have you done it already? Well, you little beauty.'

'Yes, but I need to download it onto your phone. Look, I will also need you to remove your pin number to allow me to access it.'

'Ok but I need to be there, I don't trust you Posh Boy, I don't want you stitching me up and removing my details, meet me in Association later on today, I'll have it with me. In the meantime I suggest you get on with your breakfast.'

***

'Did you enjoy your time on the wing yesterday, John?' asked Bill Gardner, who was busy writing up an overtime report for Tom Fletcher.

'Yes, it was quite an experience Bill, but I must admit I'd prefer it in the office here, I don't think I could do that job on a regular basis. I did it years ago and had quite forgotten how stressful it could be,' lied John Hughes.

'You get in the swing of it after a while, the inmates get to know you to be honest and most of them are easy to talk with. It's always strange at first. Still you probably won't have to do it again for a while and of course there was no trouble over the weekend.'

'I hope not and just pray my Christmas leave is still on,' responded John, who was now busy collating the weekend's reports.

John Hughes set about writing up the three intelligence reports he had been personally involved in from yesterday. Two were pure observations about particular prisoners who were suspected to be bullying other inmates but the third was the situation he had found himself in with Higson. He was at a cross roads on whether to even report it or should he get involved in it to see where it would lead. He decided in the end he would have to report the incident and log it with the others into the database.

***

Association in HMP Dinas Bay normally followed straight after the evening meal and the time allocated in Ridgway's view seemed to be set more for the benefit of the prison staff themselves rather than the inmates. Tim Ridgway made his way down to the meeting area and spotted Higson in deep discussion with his mates in the corner. There were only two officers on duty as far as he could see and they were busy chatting to a couple of inmates over by the pool table. He walked over and tapped Higson on the shoulder.

'Ah, Posh Boy, have you brought what you need then to complete your end of the bargain?'

'I will have if you hand me your phone, it shouldn't take me too long.'

'Ok but as discreetly as possible right, get in here now and we'll cover you,' said Higson, as he allowed Tim to come into the centre of the huddle.

'Here we are,' said Higson, as he slipped his phone into Tim's pocket.

Tim, who was now surrounded by Higson and his mates, took the phone out, switched it on and under settings selected the *Bluetooth ON* option, he did the same for his phone, paired them up and called up the folder on his phone containing the app, he pressed transfer and within a couple of minutes had transferred the software routine onto Higson's mobile.

'Ok, here it is together with a note I scribbled earlier telling you how to freeze and unfreeze the camera, it is only set to do the one in the gymnasium, alright, it won't work with any other CCTV cameras so don't bother trying it, I've no idea why you need it?'

'Great, keep it that way, that's my business so don't concern yourself with that,' said Higson, as he took the phone and the note and pocketed both of them.

'Ok, Posh Boy, I suggest you disperse now before any of the officers wonder what's going on here.'

Tim was no wiser as to why Higson needed to freeze the gymnasium CCTV but at least it had given him an idea on how he could use it as part of his own escape plan. He went over and joined Charlie who was chatting with a couple of the others.

'Getting a bit friendly now with Higson aren't you?' enquired Charlie, who was a feeling a bit put out that Tim didn't appear to be sharing information with him.

'It's nothing really, look I'll explain it all to you later when we get back to the cell, I promise,' said Tim, who had decided he had to let Charlie in on everything.

The hooter eventually went and they all returned to their cells for the night.

***

John Hughes rushed back to the caravan from the prison on the Monday evening and called up the online web meeting on the force laptop. The DCI, DS Holdsworth and Jean Price were already on the call awaiting his arrival.

'Firstly, thank you for the weekly report DC Hodgson, or should I call you Lion? Now before we ask Jean whether she has come up with any links or connections that we should be following can I ask you to please tell us more about Hywel Jones?'

'Yes, certainly sir, Hywel Jones has been with the prison service for some fifteen years, he was originally based over in Merseyside but eventually moved when Dinas Bay was built. He is a fluent Welsh speaker and a regular church goer at the local chapel. His hobbies include fishing and walking. He has been married for ten years and has four children between the ages of three and nine. He is not the most sociable man I've ever worked with, in fact he can be very difficult at times. He keeps himself to himself a lot of the time. As far as work is concerned I checked the intelligence database and discovered he managed to stop a potential riot situation breaking out about six months ago when he was temporarily assigned to the wings.'

'Thank you for that. Tell me, Jean, we haven't as yet received Hywel Jones' landline phone records but I understand you have now obtained his mobile call records, so how have you got on with those, I appreciate you haven't had much time as yet to fully analyse these?'

'Well sir, I worked through the weekend and loaded in both sets of phone transactions. I then connected them to our investigation database, I can show you now on the following screen firstly the link chart of all calls made from and to his mobile numbers. You will see that one of the mobile phone numbers is hardly used but both do connect with a mobile number on a very regular basis. I'll now switch to viewing the same data in an event chart and you can see that there are a great number of calls between the hours of 5 a.m. and 6 a.m. In fact both phones are silent between the hours of 8am and 6pm.'

'Presumably, Jean, the silent period will of course be when he is at work and is not allowed to take a mobile phone into the prison,' said DS Holdsworth.

'Yes, exactly sir, now this mobile that he is regularly calling is quite interesting,' replied Jean, moving on to the next chart and zooming in on the object.

'And why is that Jean?' asked the DCI who appreciated where the conversation was going but struggled at times with the technology.

'Well I followed it up and it belongs to a Richard Smethurst.'

'So, why is that interesting?'

'Because sir, he is the senior prison governor of HMP Dinas Bay,' chipped in John Hughes.

***

Tim had now explained to Charlie his escape plan and whilst Charlie was reluctant to get involved he realised he had no option. When all the cells were locked up for the night the two of them removed the bi-metal hacksaw blades from the spine of Tim's bible and started to saw through the three bars on the window. At first the blades made no impression whatsoever through the special coating but eventually they managed to get a groove going. At three a.m. in the morning they decided to give it a rest, returned the blades to the bible and retired to bed.

CHAPTER 20

Tuesday 8th December, 2015

Jean Price had been instructed by the DCI to find out a lot more about Hywel Jones; she had now received his bank account statements and landline phone records and she started to set about researching the links and connections across the data. Jean decided to keep a separate work file on this data to avoid confusion at a possible later date should the trail not lead anywhere. She now had a week before the next review meeting to pull together all she could find on this data. The entire investigation seemed to be focussed on Hywel Jones but deep down she now had certain misgivings about the way this was unfolding. In the meantime DS Holdsworth was tasked with investigating the lifestyle of Hywel Jones, a task which would involve him making a journey over to North Wales.

***

Higson couldn't wait to test out his new toy, the ability to freeze the CCTV in the gymnasium, so after he'd finished his day job he made his way over there followed closely by his gang of inmates. Higson stood in the doorway and made sure no one else was already in there, he pressed the phone for the app to snapshot the empty gymnasium and load the image. He had to assume it was working and the big test would come when the rest of his gang followed him in for an arranged secret meeting. He signalled to them to follow him in. They would soon know if it hadn't worked if a large number of prison officers suddenly appeared to break up the gathering.

'Right lads, welcome to our new meeting room, you know the plan, it's this Sunday, I'm expecting a drop, Morrison you know what you have to do, we are relying on you to do the business. I'll get the show on the road as arranged. Now has anyone any questions?' said Higson to the huddle of inmates.

No one uttered a word but just to be on the safe side Higson ran through the chain of events with them to avoid any confusion.

'Right, so Sunday it is, ok lads back to your cells,' said Higson after he'd finished, 'that's more than enough gym activity for today.'

He waited for the crowd to disperse and switched the CCTV image back to the live view.

***

Wednesday 9th December, 2015

DS Jim Holdsworth drove over to North Wales as soon as it was first light. Jean had booked him into a nice bed and breakfast hotel overlooking the harbour in Caernarvon for a couple of nights. This would give him plenty of time hopefully to find out a little bit more about Hywel Jones and if time permitted possibly Richard Smethurst. He needed to report back to the DCI on his return to the office on the Friday.

Jean had furnished him with as much detail on Hywel Jones as she could find online and through discreet enquiries. As expected there were a considerable number of records with that particular name mentioned online and finding the right one was easier said than done. But to make it even more difficult the man also clearly kept himself to himself and there were no social media references whatsoever. If he was a member of a local club or organisation then his name was certainly not on any website. John Hughes had at least managed to take a photograph of Hywel Jones when he was returning to his car after work. The photograph had been attached to John's latest report. After checking in at the B&B and dropping his bags off, he decided to visit the village where Hywel Jones lived, which was about three miles away overlooking the Menai Straits. He drove into the street of stone terraced houses and parked for a moment outside number 107 – Hywel's house. The large three-storey end terrace property looked as though it had been carefully looked after, in fact from the outside it was in immaculate condition; considering the time of year the small front garden could have won competitions. A paved driveway at the side of the house led to a large locked up garage. He was tempted to walk up the driveway and peer through the garage window but decided to continue to the end of the street and park up across the road from a small corner shop. In a last minute rush he had packed his bags in a hurry and only when unpacking back at the hotel had noticed he'd come without his toothbrush and toothpaste. He made his way into the shop, bought what he needed and was about to leave the shop when he noticed a number of advertisements pinned to a noticeboard on the door. His eyes were immediately focussed on one particular advertisement, an advert for car cleaning and valeting services. It wasn't the advert as such which drew his attention; it was the photograph of someone who looked just like Hywel Jones and one of the two mobile numbers that he'd been given.

***

Richard Smethurst had called for his senior officers to attend an emergency meeting in the gold conference room.

'Good morning gentlemen. You will be aware that as from tomorrow a number of prisoners will be released early on licence as part of the government directive that we received back in October. I must remind you that tomorrow is going to be a busy day for the Security Department. I also don't need to remind you that whilst everything is in place for this we do not expect any problems with the actual release arrangements. However with Christmas coming we could expect some problems from those prisoners in certain categories who are ineligible and do not qualify, therefore can I please ask you to prepare for these sorts of issues. Tom, can you please confirm all the paperwork for those who are being released will be ready?'

'Yes sir, everything is in order, all the forms are completed and the inmates will be released over a period of three hours, the inmates involved have each been given an estimated time of release,' replied Tom Fletcher, who was now looking over to the Head of Administration for the nod of agreement.

'Excellent gentlemen, well let's hope everything goes according to plan, thank you for your time.'

CHAPTER 21

Thursday 10th December, 2015

The early release program had started as planned with prisoners being released at intervals from eight a.m. The Security Department had it worked out to a fine art with paperwork and their belongings ready for each person leaving. Some of the prisoners' families had driven over to collect them but outside the prison there was also a fleet of taxis waiting to take released prisoners to the railway station. John Hughes was working with Bill Gardner and assisting with the paperwork in the back office. On more than one occasion he noticed a name he recognised from the Midshire area. It was all going smoothly until late morning, when most prisoners who were eligible had been released, when suddenly Tom Fletcher burst into the office.

'Bill, can you come quickly, a couple of the remaining prisoners have kicked off with a disturbance on 'B' wing, they are threatening the duty officer.'

'I will be with you right away sir, can you hold the fort, John?' said Bill, dashing out of the office to join Tom Fletcher.

'Yes, no problem, Bill,' came the reply.

Long before Bill and Tom Fletcher reached 'B' wing they could hear the noise from within with prisoners banging and shouting. They were shocked by what they saw as they entered the wing with five other officers, Helen Morris was being held by two inmates, Evans and Williamson. As they approached a third prisoner, Beckett, held them back and threatened them by wielding a table leg as a club. The remaining prisoners on the wing were all watching from their cell doors determined not to get involved but not wishing to miss any of the action.

'Ah, the cavalry has arrived, so you think you are all big enough do you, come on then if you want some of this, we'll soon see what you buggers are made of,' shouted Evans as he firmly pinned Helen Morris to a cell door.

'Now come on, Evans, let the officer go before this gets even more serious, you are already in enough trouble as it is,' shouted Tom Fletcher, 'we can talk about this after you have let her go, release her now.'

'We want the same rights as the inmates you've released today. Why should we have to spend Christmas in this bloody dump, it's one rule for one and one rule for another. We've all got wives and children as well, you know.'

'We can look at that as soon as you let the officer go at once. This can all be settled amicably, now put that table leg down and let the officer go immediately.'

'You'll have to fight me for it,' shouted Beckett as he wielded the club in the air.

'Look, this can all be settled calmly and quietly, we can review each of you again to see if we can release you. Now please let her go immediately,' replied Tom Fletcher.

'I don't believe you, we can hold her as long as we damn well want to.'

'Look Evans, we know you are angry and we can talk about release dates, just see sense. This is having the opposite effect.'

The officers were gradually inching further forward whilst Tom Fletcher continued talking to the ringleader Evans. Suddenly without warning and almost as if a signal had been given the officers launched into the three prisoners, releasing Helen Morris in the scuffle. She was unhurt but in a complete state of shock. The inmates themselves were now pinned to the floor by the officers as Bill Gardner grabbed the wooden table leg from Beckett.

'Are you alright, Helen?'

'Yes thanks guv, I need a strong cup of tea after that.'

'Ok, get this lot off to the segregation unit, they can calm down in there,' said Tom Fletcher, 'I'll inform the governor,' relieved that at least no one was injured.

'What about our rights?' shouted Beckett.

'Oh, yes your rights, I completely forgot about them, how silly of me, we'll remind you about those when you've had chance to calm down in the seg.'

***

Tim and Charlie had been busy every night sawing through the bars on their cell window, they only needed to saw through two which were now virtually sawn through and this would give them just about sufficient gap to squeeze through. At the end of each night they smeared black boot polish around the cuts to hide their overnight work.

They were also now collecting a large number of laundry bags and kitchen bin sacks and storing these inside their pillows in readiness for their escape. Tim had decided that Christmas Eve would be the best opportunity they would have; he had overheard one or two of the officers discussing that staff shortages would be a problem over the Christmas period and this would give him options on the route he planned to take. Tim's original plan was to escape on New Year's Eve but the progress they had made with the bars on the window meant they could go a week earlier. He had sent a text to

Alan at the Jelly Bean café with the date and time to finally put his plan into action.

***

Tom Fletcher was reviewing the audit logs for the main prisoner management system and the intelligence database. He was surprised when he saw the level of activity against Hywel Jones's username. Compared with previous months the user activity in just three weeks had increased five-fold so he decided to drill down even further to look at the actual searches that had been made. He was shocked to see that the search data on the intelligence logs alone included searches on most members of staff including governor records. He decided to tackle the problem head on and called Hywel Jones into the office.

'Hywel, I've been impressed with your workload capacity over the past month. You clearly have got to grips with the recording of intelligence reports. This is a big improvement on previous months on recording data, quite something, you must be very proud of your work rate, very productive if I may say so.'

'Thank you very much sir, I do try my best,' replied Hywel, nervously taking the credit but realising that most of this was down to John Hughes, who was still sharing his username and password.

'But there is one thing that bothers me.'

'And what is that, sir?'

'Well the audit log shows you have also been researching the data quite significantly in this last month.'

'Have I?' replied Hywel, looking somewhat surprised. 'Well, it's all part of the process sir, when an intelligence report comes in, as you know we are trained to refer to other previous instances by looking at historic reports.'

'But why would you research the prison governor records? Is there something you are not telling me, Hywel?'

'No, sir, I didn't think I had been researching that data.'

'Ah, but you have, it's all here in this audit report that I'm looking at.'

'Well there must be a mistake, the computer must have made an error,' said Hywel, who had suddenly realised that John Hughes had also been performing detailed research using the same login details.

'No mistake Hywel, the computer hasn't made an error. So I ask you again why would you be looking at data involving the governor?'

'I don't know sir, I can't explain it.'

'Well I'm passing this up to the governors to decide on whether you should be suspended or not, in the meantime I suggest you return to your desk and get on with the work you are supposed to be doing.'

CHAPTER 22

Saturday 12th December, 2015

John Hughes had been up early on the Saturday morning, he had already submitted his weekly report to Midshire Police in readiness for their weekly meeting. He'd decided he would have a day to himself today, the weather was fine after the recent storms and he thought he would get some exercise and walk part of the Lleyn Peninsular coastal path. So packing a flask, fleece, waterproofs, rucksack and walking boots he firstly drove over to the village of Trefor, parked up in the village car park, donned his walking boots and set off across the cliff top walk. The path was still extremely slippery after the heavy rains and he had to take care on some of the inclines. There was not a soul in sight and it was wonderful to be out in the fresh sea air, it was clearly a place where he could think and breathe. All that could be heard was the continuous squawking and wailing of the seagulls overhead.

As he rounded the corner of the coastal headland he came across the delightfully old and unspoilt St. Bueno's church at Pistyll, which was resting in a gentle hollow. He pushed open the creaking door and rested for a while, sitting in the oak pews amongst the rushes and sweetly smelling herbs which were carefully strewn across the floor. This was truly a magical place for reflection and it seemed a million miles away from the prison environment he had recently become accustomed to. He thought back to how life had been before he foolishly took on this assignment. He badly missed his wife and family and he was thinking of ways to make up for his weeks of absence, he couldn't wait to get home and spend Christmas with them. In just under two weeks' time he would be at home in front of the fire, watching the children opening their presents on Christmas morning. It was so restful in this place and he thought back to all the Christmases they had enjoyed together. He sat back thinking and day dreaming of those wonderful times and would have stayed longer but the walk and lunch eventually beckoned.

He continued with his journey across the clifftops, taking in the breath taking views over the Irish Sea, and decided to spend a leisurely lunch down at the delightful Ty Coch (Red House) pub on the beach at Porthdinllaen. Refreshed and ready to continue, he strolled past the splendid new lifeboat station which stood proudly at the end of the beach before heading back along the deserted shoreline. It was now getting dusk and already the storm clouds were gathering on the horizon. He quickened his pace, climbing upwards through the windswept gorse-lined path on the cliffs. He was now just about a mile away from where he had parked when he noticed a flash of light out at sea. He watched and waited, there it was again; a small fishing boat flashing a torch light and making its way into the shore below him. He stopped and thought it strange. There was no landing jetty near here and he presumed the boat may have possibly got into some sort of difficulty. He stood on the clifftop and watched as the little boat anchored just offshore. To his surprise he could then see two figures appear from behind a large rock. He watched as they waded out to meet the boat. John couldn't make out how many were in the boat but he could see them now handing what looked like boxes out as the two people waded in alongside the boat. He decided to make his way down the path to try and get a clearer view. He could now see a man and a woman carrying the boxes onto the pebble beach. The wind was now getting up and he could just about hear their voices but couldn't quite make out what was actually being said. He took out his notebook and scribbled in the semi darkness the only words he could barely hear which seemed to be repeated, the name "Gwen" and "unease". The little fishing boat had now left and was no longer in sight. John kept still, waiting for the couple below him to make their way up the rough carved out stone steps to a layby in the lane. He watched and waited as they loaded the boxes into the dark coloured Land Rover. Minutes later they were gone.

About an hour later John was back in the warmth of the caravan thinking on how best to follow this up.

Sunday 13th December, 2015

The Reverend Philip Graham had been appointed to HM prisons in the region as the visiting Church of England preacher for the pre-Christmas period. He arrived at HMP Dinas Bay visitor centre early, in readiness for the Sunday morning service. It was not a prison he'd been to before and had been impressed with the building and the welcome he got when checking in at reception. He made his way through into the chapel, accompanied by a prison officer, and was surprised and delighted to see that the pews were almost full. He had been told that attendance for Sunday worship was not as it should be and he thought maybe word has got around about the sermons he delivered. The service started with the hymn "Onward Christian Soldiers" and whilst the performance was not as tuneful as it could have been at least it was rousing to say the least.

The reverend had just completed his sermon on forgiveness and was about to announce to the congregation the next hymn when he was suddenly interrupted by an inmate who leapt from his seat in the front pew.

'That's easy for you to say, Reverend, but how can we forgive those when we are treated like animals, isn't that right lads, animals, sodding animals?' shouted Higson, as he grabbed the microphone from the vicar.

'We are treated like bloody animals, hear, hear,' shouted one of the prisoners in the congregation.

'If you treat us like pigs then we'll bloody well act like pigs,' came another one of the voices.

'So, what are we going to do about it boys!' shouted Higson.

'Rebel, rebel, let's teach the buggers a lesson,' came the response.

'Give them a dose of their own medicine, see how they like it.'

The inmates were now on their feet shouting and bawling, sometimes directly at each other.

'Now come on lads, please sit down. Come on now be reasonable, this is no way to behave in God's house,' replied the reverend, who was now anxiously trying to make his voice heard above the din. The reverend was now in a complete state of shock and he had never experienced a response like this to any of his sermons.

The three prison officers who were on duty at the door came to the reverend's rescue and one of them grabbed the microphone from Higson and pleaded for them to calm down, but the crowd were by now throwing hymn books at the officers standing in the front of the chapel. The reverend was safely escorted by one of the prison officers out of the chapel away from the noise and into the safety of the visitor area.

By now other prison officers were arriving on the scene and they decided to contain the problem in the chapel by locking the doors but they hadn't noticed that one particular prisoner sitting at the back had already left in the mayhem.

***

John Hughes was looking forward to his lie in on the Sunday morning, he had planned a restful day, relaxing in the morning, more than likely ending up watching the football on the TV and then enjoying a late Sunday roast washed down with a couple of nice pints at the Smithy Arms. He thought what more could a man ask for. As he dozed off, however, his plans for the day were soon shattered when he received a phone call mid-morning from Tom Fletcher.

'John, I'm really sorry to trouble you on your weekend off but we have a problem on our hands, we have a riot on 'A' wing which is getting out of control and we need as many officers who are currently on leave to return to the prison as soon as possible to make sure it doesn't get out of hand on the other wings.'

'When and where did this start?'

'In the prison chapel, right in the middle of the morning service, can you please get over here as quickly as possible?'

'Yes, no problem sir, I'll be with you as soon as I can,' said John, as he dashed out of bed and headed for the bathroom, thirty minutes later he was driving into the prison car park.

***

The two young men hid behind the disused upturned boat on the beach below. They waited patiently for the confirmation text; as soon as it arrived they switched on the drone and steered it upwards into the air above and guided it swiftly over the prison boundary wall. They watched on the tiny hand-held screen as the remote camera transmitted the live images of the prison exercise yard. They didn't have to wait long as their contact soon came into view and then carefully they glided the drone towards him landing it softly onto the hard concrete yard below. The parcel was carefully unloaded and the drone took to the air once again returning like an obedient animal to its owner.

***

'Glad you could make it, John,' said Tom Fletcher as John Hughes entered the security office. 'We've managed to contain them within the chapel at present and hopefully with the minimum of damage. The chapel is one of the few places we have no CCTV camera so we've no idea if they have been damaging the place but we decided to let them calm down for an hour or so. They'll be getting hungry about then and ready for their lunch which might make it easier when we re-enter the chapel. We know who the ringleaders are and our first priority is to bang them up in the segregation unit,' he continued.

'Don't tell me sir, it's Higson and Brown,' replied John, taking a seat at his desk.

'Bang on John, how on earth did you guess?'

'No guess sir, the intel has been pointing at those two for weeks.'

***

He grabbed hold of the small parcel and stuffed it under his jumper, he then made his way from the exercise yard across into 'A' wing and handed it over to Morrison, who was sitting patiently waiting in his cell for its safe arrival. It was now safely inserted through the slit in the back of the mattress.

***

'Right chaps, we've given them an hour, let's go down and inspect the damage,' said Tom Fletcher to the officers that he had called back in from leave.

The twelve officers led by Tom Fletcher made their way down to the chapel and joined the other officers who were now waiting patiently by the locked door.

'Well, it seems peaceful enough in there to me, I can't hear anything,' said Tom Fletcher to one of the officers guarding the door.

'Yes, we haven't heard anything for the past half an hour, so in we go chaps, but be prepared just in case, it could be a trap.'

The officer immediately in front of the door unlocked it and the officers piled in there. To their complete amazement all the inmates were sitting in the pews either chatting amongst themselves or just reading, almost as if they were waiting for the Sunday service to start. The hymn books were all back in their places and there was no visible damage whatsoever.

'Ok, gentlemen, the service is over. I use the term gentlemen very cautiously. I hope you lot have had time to calm down from your disgraceful behaviour. Now form an orderly queue and make your way back to your cells. Apart from you pair, Higson and Brown, you can come with us. You are on report for organising this disturbance and are destined for the "seg", with a bit of luck you might be out of there back in your cells for Christmas,' shouted Tom Fletcher, pointing to two prison officers to lead them away.

'Let's hope it was worth it,' Arthur Higson said laughingly as he nodded to Alan Brown as they were personally escorted out of the chapel, en route to the segregation unit.

The remaining inmates were led away back to their cells mumbling and laughing whilst those officers who were recalled from leave returned home.

CHAPTER 23

Monday 14th December, 2015

'How many hours overtime can I put down for yesterday boss? I was only here about two hours,' said John Hughes, who was busy filling out his timesheet.

'Yeah, I'm sorry about that, we thought we had a real problem on our hands. It could have got quite ugly. You should be ok for claiming four hours, it's the least we can do for disturbing your weekend,' replied Tom Fletcher, who was updating the whiteboard.

'Well to be honest it didn't disrupt it too much, I needed to get up out of bed, if you hadn't called me I think I'd have still have been there at lunchtime. How bad was it in the end?'

'Potentially it could have been a lot worse and I know the governor is far from happy with the current staff resources he has available. It beats me what the buggers were up to yesterday. There is more to this than meets the eye you know, we clearly had an idea that some of them are unhappy about the early release programme after the issues on Thursday but the chapel was packed out and seemed prepared for this. The Sunday service had never seen so many attendees, although I do remember...'

At that point Tom Fletcher's personal radio went off.

'Tom, it's Richard Smethurst, can you please come up to see me in the next five minutes. I wish to hold an urgent meeting with all the heads of department.'

'Will do sir,' replied Tom, switching his radio off.

'I must go gentlemen, as you heard the governor has requested I attend a meeting,' said Tom, leaving the office hurriedly.

'I wonder what that's about?' said Ian. 'He normally gives them all plenty of notice for briefings in the calendar.'

'Search me, he probably wants to brief everyone on the events of yesterday I guess, particularly the lessons learnt I would imagine,' said Bill.

But John remained silent, he had an idea on what was possibly about to come.

***

The heads of departments were all gathered around the conference table in the meeting room, having been called in at a moment's notice. The senior prison governor, Richard Smethurst, had just arrived and sat down to chair the meeting.

'Firstly thank you everyone for attending this impromptu meeting at such short notice. As to the reason for calling this meeting, you know over the past few days we have had some worrying disturbances within the prison. Yesterday particularly in the chapel we witnessed some disgraceful behaviour in the Sunday morning service. I really must write to apologise to the Reverend for the whole sorry incident. Fortunately this didn't develop into a full-scale riot and I'd like to put on record my personal thanks to those officers who dealt with the incident so efficiently and effectively. I'd also like to thank those officers who returned from being on leave. I really do appreciate their help. I trust you will thank them personally on my behalf. Fortunately there was no damage done to the chapel. However this leaves us with a potential headache on staffing the prison over the Christmas period and I have decided that we have no choice but to cancel leave for those officers who would normally be working. This clearly excludes those who have booked holidays several months in advance. Can you please therefore brief your appropriate teams of my decision? Now are there are any questions?'

'Yes, are we to assume this includes all civilian staff such as canteen, cleaners, etc. sir?' asked Tom Kinsey, the Head of Administration.

'No, this just affects the operational and security officers, I'm sure we can manage on the catering and cleaning side,' replied the governor.

'If I may say so, and with great respect sir, this is not going to go down well with the officers, particularly those who came to our rescue over the weekend,' remarked Tom Fletcher.

'Yes, I realise that Tom, but we don't really have any choice in the matter. Now if that's all can we please get back to the job in hand? Thank you for your time, gentlemen.'

***

'Good morning Jean, have you organised the online meeting for tonight?' asked DS Holdsworth.

'Yes, it's all in hand sarge, the meeting is set for the same time as last week,' replied Jean, who had just arrived in the office. 'Did you have a nice time in North Wales? I was off on Friday and missed your return.'

'I did indeed thank you Jean, it was a bit wet but amazingly mild for the time of year.'

'What was the B&B like, the one that I booked for you? It looked pretty good on their website.'

'Yes it was very comfortable thanks, great views and definitely one for including in the recommended accommodation handbook. I've got quite a few notes to write up following my visit and I'll go through these at the meeting, but I think we may be barking up the wrong tree. I'm personally not convinced about our Mr Hywel Jones.'

'Yes, interesting you say that as I'm in agreement, I can't find anything to take this any further. We could start looking at his emails but I think we may be wasting our time.'

'Well, I'm sure we can cover our next moves with the DCI later tonight.'

***

'Surely you are not serious! You are bleeding joking sir, aren't you?' shouted John Hughes, losing his temper across the other side of the office.

'No, it's not a joke I'm afraid, John, we will need all the officers we can get in over the Christmas period. The governor himself will also be coming in to make sure things go as smoothly as possible.'

'Well, my family are going to be very upset at this I can tell you, I mean as you know I don't see them as often as other officers at present as I'm working away. Is there anything you can possibly do to exclude me from these arrangements?'

Tom Fletcher hadn't seen John Hughes like this, it was a side of him he'd not witnessed before and he was surprised and somewhat annoyed at the anger that John was now showing.

'No, I'm afraid not John, every one of us including myself will be required. Can I suggest that perhaps you have a couple of days off this week and take a long weekend? Treat it as a sort of pre-Christmas few days with them before the event. It's not ideal, of course.'

'Well that's better than nothing I suppose, but it's not going to go down well, I am far from happy with this, as you can gather, boss.'

'None of us are happy with this situation, John, but we will have to make the best of it. We all realised that we could get called upon like this from time to time when we first joined the prison service. You must remember that at your induction process.'

John Hughes thought about responding to this but decided he had to maintain his silence.

***

Arthur Higson and Geoff Brown had now been placed in the segregation unit and not for the first time. The "Seg" or the "Block" as it is known, is like a prison within a prison, a very lonely place, a place where prisoners only come out typically for one hour a day's exercise and the remaining twenty-three hours they are locked up. No TV, no personal possessions, meals served along the floor and no communication.

But Higson had got used to his own company, he'd been here several times before and it was the promise of getting access to the package that had just been brought in that kept him thinking positive.

***

Hywel Jones had been recalled into Tom Fletcher's office.

'Please come in, Hywel, and take a seat. The governor and I have now had time to consider the fact that you have been researching the intelligence database for various staff records, including searching for anything connected with the governor himself. Whilst we appreciate it is part of your role to analyse the incident reports, we find it odd that you have been looking at certain records which have no bearing on current activity within the prison, and under normal circumstances we would suspend you pending further investigation. However we have decided that on this occasion we will issue you with a warning which will be on your personnel record. I suggest therefore that you return to your desk but remember we have a secure audit log monitoring system in place and we will be watching for any repeat of this behaviour. Do you have anything to say?'

'No, nothing at all, sir, other than that I can assure you that it won't be happening again.'

Hywel Jones was mystified why John Hughes had been clearly researching personal staff data and to make it worse, under his username and password, but he knew he had only himself to blame for not passing on the correct login details. He left Tom Fletcher's office, made his way into the Security office and returned to his desk. He opened the top drawer of the desk and took out a slip of paper which he had had for some weeks. He walked over to John Hughes's desk and handed it over to him personally with the words, 'Here we are, this is your username and password that you should be using from now on.'

***

John Hughes needed a drink badly, he'd had a terrible day in work with the news that he would have to work through Christmas and he wasn't sure how he could even bring himself to ring Sue to give her the news. He would have normally called into the Smithy Arms on his way home to drown his sorrows but he had no choice but to rush back to the caravan for his online meeting with Midshire Police. He was certainly not in the best frame of mind for an online meeting with DCI Bentley and the team.

He parked up and entered the caravan; it was bitterly cold and he turned the gas fire on full. He just had enough time to make himself a quick cup of tea and go into the bedroom to login and connect to the online meeting. The team back in Midshire were already online, sitting and waiting patiently in DS Holdsworth's office.

'Good evening Jack, I'm glad you could make the call, it's been a busy day for you as usual I imagine,' said the DCI, dispensing with using Jack's undercover name.

'Good evening all,' replied John Hughes. 'I assume you have all received my latest report?'

'Yes, we have indeed,' replied the DCI, 'but before we get onto that I'd like to recap with the actions that were placed on DS Holdsworth and Jean Price at our last meeting. Firstly DS Holdsworth, you have made a brief trip over to North Wales to see what you could uncover regarding Hywel Jones and time permitting possibly the prison governor Richard Smethurst. So what did you discover?'

'Well sir, as you know I made the journey over to Caernarvon and firstly drove round to the area where Hywel lives. I discovered that Hywel is running a part time business in car valeting in his spare time. He has a wife and four children to support and I have no reason to believe he is conducting any other form of business. He is friendly with Richard Smethurst the prison governor as they both belong to the local ramblers group; Richard is the chairman and Hywel is the secretary, which explains somewhat why they would be having regular phone communication with each other. In asking discreetly around the neighbourhood about Hywel, he is very well thought about, a quiet family man who keeps himself to himself. He is also a regular churchgoer and a chorister in a local male voice choir. I believe they are a very good choir.'

'Yes, I'm sure they are and thank you for that Jim, that is most interesting. Jean, how did you get on with analysing Mr Jones's bank account and landline records?'

'Well, nothing special sir, not a great deal in the bank account statements, he appears to be living month to month, no great income and expenditure to report on, just his salary going in each month and the usual bills being paid regularly,' replied Jean, handing over the transaction charts to the DCI.

'So, it appears that we have been barking up the wrong tree. I'd appreciate your thoughts, Jack?'

'Well, I'm lost for words sir, all I can say is that there seemed to be something fishy about the man, particularly when overhearing his phone conversation.'

'Well, I imagine DC Hodgson you overheard someone chasing up his order for car cleaning materials, not exactly a crime as I'm sure you'll agree!' replied the DCI sarcastically, as he looked around at the rest of the team in the office.

'No sir, I agree,' responded John Hughes, 'it appears I may have made a mistake.'

'An expensive mistake at that, well team we seem to have wasted considerable time and effort in following this line of enquiry, here we are six weeks on since we took this investigation on and we are no further forward, so what do you suggest now?'

'Well sir, we could follow the Higson activity, he seemed to be earmarked as a troublemaker in 'A' wing,' said DS Holdsworth, who was looking to take some of the attention away from DC Hodgson.

'Yes, well I have some news on Higson which I'm sure DC Hodgson is probably aware of. According to a call I received from HMP HQ this morning it appears he started a riot in the prison yesterday morning. Our friend Higson is now banged up in the Segregation Unit. Isn't that so, DC Hodgson?'

'Yes, it is sir, a number of officers including myself were brought back in over the weekend to deal with it,' he replied.

'Admirable, I'm sure, so why weren't we watching Higson instead of chasing after this Jones fella.'

'Well, I didn't think Higson would be worth bothering with at this stage, Hywel Jones seemed like a good lead at the time, sir.'

'A good lead, we wasted man hours and effort in following that up.'

'Well it's all I could find out within the time and with all respect it was early days, sir.'

'Well personally DC Hodgson I think it's Ridgway who we should be watching, I've said so all along and I think we would be best focussing on him. I don't know what he's planning but he's a clever bugger and you can bet your bottom dollar it'll involve technology of some sort, that young man could cause untold damage if he's let loose. For all I know he could be hacking into the prison network as we speak.'

'With the greatest respect sir, I think that is rubbish, I don't believe Ridgway is involved here, as I say he wasn't even in the prison when we were first alerted, granted he might have got involved in whatever is going on in there at present but I feel there are other inmates involved in this.'

'We mustn't lose sight of the fact that our informant believes whatever is happening in there will have repercussions on a grander scale. So what exactly do you think is involved in there, DC Hodgson?' snapped the DCI who was now becoming more and more aggressive.

Jack Hodgson drew in a deep breath. 'Well, I'm not sure but I think contraband is involved, maybe on a large scale, a very large scale, exactly what I don't know.'

'Contraband, but what have the riots got to do with this?'

'I think that could have been a smoke screen, sir?' replied John Hughes, who was now tiring of the whole conversation.

'A smoke screen! Well I'm fast losing patience here DC Hodgson, and I suggest that you get back in there and provide us with far better intelligence, because up until now you have given us nothing worthwhile to go on. You need to get back in there smartish and discover what exactly is being planned there. You can start by providing us with more information on Ridgway and his connections. He was a devious little bastard and I've never forgiven him for what he did to an old friend of mine, Superintendent Alan Jackson, planting pornography on his laptop.'

'That will be a complete waste of time, sir.'

'Are you refusing to follow this line of enquiry, officer?'

'Yes sir, I suppose I am, I don't believe it's the right approach and that's another thing, I do need some time off away from there, I'm hoping I can at least get back to my family for Christmas.'

'Well, I tell you what DC Hodgson,' shouted DCI Bentley as he headed for the door, 'I'll make it easy for you, as from today you are suspended from duty for insolence and refusing to obey an order. DS Holdsworth please come to my office in the morning to discuss our next steps and close down that bloody online link, I'm out of here before I say something I shouldn't.'

But John Hughes had already closed down his online connection and was on his way to the pub.

***

Tim Ridgway was busy in his cell drawing a diagram on a scrap of paper.

'What are you doing, Tim?' asked Charlie, who was now showing a little more interest in escaping from the prison.

'I'm sketching out a plan of the prison, well as much a plan as I can make out. I've managed to get an aerial view of the prison online on my phone using the free internet mapping tools that are available. From here I can see that these are the CCTV camera positions and I've got to work out which ones we need to freeze on our escape route.'

'But you don't know the numbers of them.'

'Yes, but if we are careful enough we can get those on the fly.'

'On the fly, that's risky, you are joking of course, it'll be in the middle of the night.'

'No, as long as we keep out of their vision and range we should be able to get close enough underneath them to shine a light upwards and jot the asset number down. I can then freeze that IP address, it's easy. I think we are looking at two CCTV positions.'

'Hang on, what do you mean shine a light? You are forgetting something aren't you, we don't have a torch or is this something on your Christmas present wish list off Higson,' he remarked sarcastically.

'No, I don't need Higson for this. We do have a torch, my smart phone remember has a torch app, it will be fully charged in readiness.'

'Bloody brilliant.'

'Let's hope it is.'

CHAPTER 24

Tuesday 15th December, 2015

'I've just had John Hughes on the phone, he's called in sick so you will have to do the best you can today chaps,' said Tom Fletcher, entering the Security office.

'Did he say when he might be back in, as we have quite a backlog of incident reports to get through after the disturbances last weekend?' asked Bill Gardner, who was now looking concerned at the mounting pile of paperwork in John's tray.

'No, he didn't but as long as he is back here in time over Christmas we should be ok. We are going to need all the staff resources we can get. I think he may have taken my suggestion about having a few days off with his family. I can't blame him really. It can't be easy working and living away from your family, particularly at this time of the year as I'm sure you'll all agree.'

***

John Hughes had been up early on the Tuesday morning, he'd packed his bags and was at last looking forward to at least getting back to his family. He was still annoyed at the heated discussion he had had with the DCI and felt if the meeting had been face to face it wouldn't have got out of hand as it did. He unplugged the laptop equipment and placed everything into their carrying cases. He had decided to leave some of his clothes and provisions in the caravan as he planned to return later. As far as he was concerned the job was far from over and he intended to get to the bottom of this investigation if only to prove the DCI wrong. He had just finished loading the bags in the boot and was just about to drive away when around the corner came the familiar figure of Edward Jones.

'Ah, Bore Da, good morning Mr Hughes, not a bad morning, I understand you are leaving us and I see you are packed up already to get on your way. Are you off now for Christmas?'

'I am indeed, Mr Jones, but I'll be back hopefully before the New Year. I've locked everything up now, it's all switched off so Merry Christmas to you and your family, I really must be on my way.'

'And Nadolig Llawen to you and your family, I look forward to seeing you soon. Bye for now, have a good one.'

John Hughes drove out of the caravan park but suddenly thought back to the conversation he'd just had with Edward. How did Mr Jones know that he was leaving, he used the words "understand you're leaving." He quickly dismissed the thought, he'd probably seen him packing the car anyway. John Hughes was soon on his way home as Jack Hodgson but not before he'd switched cars again and dropped off all the laptop equipment with Jean at Divisional HQ.

***

DS Holdsworth was deep in conversation with DCI Bentley, discussing how they could continue with the undercover investigation at HMP Dinas Bay.

'Having slept on it maybe I was a little hasty with Jack Hodgson,' said the DCI, 'but to be honest we didn't seem to be getting anywhere and the Detective Chief Superintendent had already started to give me grief.'

'Well, it was a difficult conversation sir,' replied DS Holdsworth, who was trying to be as diplomatic as possible. 'Jack means well of course but what do you think we should tell the prison?'

'I think we keep quiet about it for the time being, I'll inform the HMP HQ intelligence section to say that our man has a long term illness and won't be coming back there and they will do the rest but as far as the prison itself is concerned we don't say anything to them. I don't suppose you fancy doing any undercover work, Jim?'

'No, afraid not sir, those days are well and truly gone. I do have one idea sir, which might be worth considering. When Jean and I were looking through the list of prisoners from our area I couldn't help noticing one in particular, the name Billy Grant. You might recall Billy, who was sentenced to five years for defrauding local investors through a so-called hedge fund he'd concocted. Unless they've moved him he was on the same wing as Ridgway.'

'Yes, I remember Billy Grant, he was an informant a few years back, I'd forgotten all about him, bloody hell Billy Grant, a right slimy little bugger.'

'Well Billy is still in prison there and I knew him quite well as an informant, I was his handler as a matter of fact for a few years. I think he might be prepared to assist us again. It will cost us of course but at least we might get to know what on earth is going on in there, purely from a prisoner's perspective that is.'

'Great idea Jim, set up a visiting order and get over to see him as soon as possible. We need to keep our eye on Mr Ridgway.'

***

Wednesday 16th December, 2015

Sue Hodgson was delighted to have her husband back home. It came as quite a surprise when Jack, still sporting the beard, turned up the previous afternoon unannounced. The children arriving back from school later that day were over the moon when they walked into the kitchen to see their father back again. As little Emily said this is the best early Christmas present she'd ever had. The house looked splendid, it was decorated throughout, the tree was up, the log burner was lit and everything was ready for Christmas. Jack thought how good it was to be home at last, reunited with his family, back in his own bed and away from the prison. All he wanted to do now was to shave off the beard, forget all about HMP Dinas Bay and enjoy life with the family once again.

Jack and Sue had stayed up late the previous night discussing everything that had happened family wise whilst he had been away. They steered clear of Jack's so-called course in North Wales. Jack had a lot of catching up to do and told Sue that he now had time off in lieu at present but he didn't wish to tell her that he was now under suspension. She could tell something had been going on but living with a policeman most of her life she knew better not to pry.

***

Billy Grant was working in the prison kitchens preparing lunch when prison officer Henderson came in with a note for him.

'Grant, you have a visitor booked in for Saturday afternoon, I presume you know about this?'

'Visitor! I don't get any visitors, you must be mistaking me for someone else.'

'You are Billy Grant, aren't you, well an old friend of yours, his name is Jim Holdsworth, is coming to visit you,' replied Henderson, thrusting the note at him.

Billy caught on quickly, he'd remembered Jim from his past, they had got on well together, he thought perhaps it's time for a bit of business again.

'Oh, right, yes Jim, I forgot I'd asked him to visit,' replied Billy, 'yeah, Saturday afternoon, looking forward to it.' He thought to himself, I wonder what he's after.

***

Jack Hodgson was enjoying his time at home but try as he might he couldn't get Dinas Bay out of his mind. He sat in his favourite armchair going through his scribbled notes and reflected on each situation. The approach made to him by Higson for him to earn a fast buck; Greg Henderson's possible involvement; was Hywel Jones really whiter than white?; was Ridgway involved in this lot after all; what about the little fishing boat and the boxes that were transported to the Land Rover. All of this had to be connected somehow or was it; was he trying to piece together an impossible unconnected jigsaw. He decided for the time being he would try and relax and enjoy Christmas but he promised himself that after Boxing Day he would return to the caravan.

CHAPTER 25

Saturday 19th December, 2015

DS Holdsworth drove over to North Wales and arrived at HMP Dinas Bay in plenty of time for visiting. He took a seat in the visitors' waiting room surrounded by families of inmates all wishing to see their loved ones. This would be the last weekend before Christmas and the room was full. One by one they were called into the security vetting area to have their paperwork checked and then to be searched prior to entering the large visitor meeting area.

Finally it was Jim's turn and he made his way through to his allocated table 18 and waited for Billy Grant to appear. It had been almost ten years since Jim last met him. Billy was then a young teenager who had been mixing with all the wrong types. He somehow had got himself involved from shoplifting and into a gang who were stealing cars and joyriding around the Wilmslow area. This had developed into breaking and entering and Billy had provided some useful information on the gang leaders.

Jim was amazed when Billy eventually arrived; he'd lost weight, his head was shaven and he was now sporting a couple of tattoos on his neck.

'Hello Billy, it's been a long time, how are you keeping?' said Jim, standing up to greet him.

'Hello Mr Holdsworth, fancy you coming over to see me, this is a pleasant surprise.'

'It's Jim, Billy call me Jim, Mr Holdsworth makes me feel old. Can I get you a coffee or a tea?' asked Jim, pointing to the vending machines on the far wall.

'Yes, that would be good, er Jim, coffee, two sugars please and a chocolate bar.'

Jim went over and got the drinks and chocolate, the two of them sat down to chat.

'Well as I say this is a surprise, what brings you over here, how can I help you?' enquired Billy in a hushed voice.

'Well Billy, we believe there maybe something big being organised here, we don't know what it is but we believe it involves the outside world on a grand scale, a sort of network of connections. You're a sharp cookie, we were wondering whether you were aware of anything.'

Billy took a sharp intake of breath. 'Well I'm not aware of anything and of course this sort of information costs.'

'Yes, I thought it might come down to money. We can sort something for you on that if that helps.'

'Well not necessarily money, I mean if I could get an earlier release, possibly on licence, by helping you perhaps?'

'Well that may be more difficult but yes, let me see what I can come up with, you'll have to trust me though and it may take a bit of time.'

'I trust you Mr Holdsworth, sorry I mean Jim. Yes I'll keep my ear to the ground and report back to you at various times. I will call you to arrange another meeting if I hear anything.'

'Well to be honest Billy, we were hoping you might have some information today, for example have you come across an inmate called Tim Ridgway or Charlie Ellis?'

'Yes, they are on the same wing as me, I work with Charlie in the kitchen, he's a decent enough bloke. He shares a cell with Tim Ridgway, he's a quiet sort of a lad, not much to say about him really.'

'Yes, that's the guy, well do you know whether Ridgway has been up to anything?'

'Well I know he's got some skills that have been asked for by Higson. Arthur Higson is a nasty bit of work on the same landing as us.'

'Really, which skills are those?'

'Well as I understand it, this Ridgway's a bit of a whizz kid on computers and things, I must confess I don't know anything about them. My mother always told me, stick to what you know son and that's what I always say.'

'Computer skills eh, well that's interesting, I don't suppose you know what Higson is up to?'

'No, as I say Higson is a nasty piece of work, he's the guy who can seem to get anything smuggled in here. He once managed to bring a budgie in for one inmate, they soon found that I can tell you, it was chirping away in the bloke's cell.'

'Fascinating, it puts a whole new meaning on budgie smugglers!' laughed Jim. 'Anyway, look this has been useful Billy, I'll see what I can do about an early release, I can't promise of course but I will do my best. In the meantime keep an eye on Ridgway, I'll call in again after Christmas to see if there's an update. It's been good to see you after all this time. I'll be off now, it's a long drive back to Manchester. Goodbye for now Billy.'

'Goodbye Mr Holdsworth, sorry I mean Jim.'

***

It was a bright but bitterly cold, wet and windy Christmas Eve morning in HMP Dinas Bay, there was no chance of a white Christmas and in some ways it was still one of the mildest on record.

The prison at the best of times could feel like a lonely and isolated place but at Christmas it became even worse. For some this would be the first Christmas they would spend away from their loved ones and prisoners were now also not allowed to receive presents as a matter of security. There was no visiting on Christmas Eve or Christmas Day but all preparations were now in hand for the day itself. Christmas lunch was well planned and it would be served in the canteens as normal but prisoners would be allowed to take theirs back to their own cells if they so preferred. The prison officers were also doing their best to brighten the mood in the prison by organising quizzes for inmates, running pool tournaments and extending their hours of association. Tim Ridgway on the one hand had other activities on his mind and was now putting the final touches to his escape plan. He had called Alan at the Jelly Bean café from the pin phone on the wall of the wing just to check whether he had received his text messages and to ensure that everything would be in place at the agreed time. Alan confirmed that it was all systems go and not to panic.

The governor, Richard Smethurst, through recalling certain officers had managed to maintain the staffing levels over the holiday and after the riots and disturbances earlier in the month the prison had settled down once again. As dusk fell Tim and Charlie sat in their cell going over in detail each step of the plan and double checking that they had everything they needed. They had decided that rather than wait until midnight they would make their escape following the lock up of cells for the night while prisoners were still watching TV and listening to loud music.

At 9pm they decided to make their move. Charlie slowly and carefully removed the bars from the cell window which by now were only being held together by chewing gum. Tim turned the TV volume up and then covering the glass with an old polo shirt proceeded to smash it on the outside using one of the iron bars. The loud music from surrounding cells assisted them by masking the noise and the glass eventually shattered. They picked out and removed the broken glass carefully to give them just enough room to squeeze out of the broken window. Charlie had previously tied together the sturdy laundry bags using the black kitchen bags as string. He tied the first laundry bag to the remains of a bar still embedded in the window ledge and slowly let out the length of bags. Tim was first out and abseiled down the thirty foot drop to the slate roof below. Charlie followed him and they quietly edged their way across the roof top.

'Ok Charlie, this is the first CCTV camera, stay in the shadow and shine the light upwards directly underneath it. Tell me what the number is that you can see,' whispered Tim, who was ready to make a note of the asset number.

'It's asset number 31745, at least I think it looks like a 5 from here it might be a 3,' replied Charlie, who was straining his eyes to read it.

Tim quickly brought up the list on his phone. 'Yes it is a 5, there aren't any cameras with that other number.'

He tapped in the number on the app, pressed the freeze button and reset the image on the security monitor.

'Great, this is where we test the cameras again; hopefully it's the same as the gymnasium. We'll soon find out if the alarm goes off!' said Tim. 'Come on follow me as quietly as you can.'

They moved across into the CCTV range and prayed that the app was doing its job. As they moved onto the wall above the exercise yard they could see a further camera which was placed at eye level from where they stood. They slowly crawled over to the camera, repeated the asset check, tapped in the number and froze the image. They moved steadily forward and were now on the very edge of the exercise yard wall. Tim carefully snipped through the rolls of barbed wire on the top of the wall and they could now see the drop below was about twenty feet to the top of the rocky outcrop below.

'How the hell are we going to get down there? If we jump onto that lot we'll be crippled!' cried Charlie. 'We've no more laundry bags and there is nothing to tie them to even if we did have.'

217

Tim shone the light towards the end of the rocks.

'If you look just to the right at the far end of the wall, below there are the remains of an old tree surrounded by gorse bushes, our best bet is to edge along a bit and jump into the bushes to the right of that and just hope for the best.'

'Bloody hell Tim, we could get killed, never mind get cut to ribbons.'

'It's a chance we'll have to take.'

They slowly crept along the top of the wall.

'I'll go first,' said Tim, and without any further warning edged his way across and jumped down into the prickly gorse.

'Are you alright Tim?' whispered Charlie from above.

'Yeah, apart from lots of scratches, I think you'll find it will save your fall, give me a minute and I'll move out of the way.'

Next thing Charlie crawled nervously across, jumped and sure enough the gorse played its part.

The two of them made their way down and clambered over the rocks and down onto the pebble and shingle beach below. Tim flashed his torch light out to sea twice, there was nothing but complete darkness and he panicked for a moment; he thought maybe Alan had forgotten to arrange the boat pickup. And then suddenly out of the gloom came a single solitary light.

'That's them,' said Tim excitedly, and provided a further flash of light in acknowledgement. 'They are on the way, come on let's walk further down towards the shoreline.'

Five minutes later the small fishing boat came into view; it had now cut its engine and was moored about fifty yards off shore.

'Come on then Charlie, I hope your swimming has improved.'

'You are joking Tim, aren't you?'

'Yes of course I am, we only have to wade out to it, it's probably only up to waist height.'

Soon they were being hauled into the boat by two complete strangers. They were cold and wet but ready for the next part of their journey across the choppy Irish Sea. The conditions were challenging to say the least as the little boat pitched and lurched from side to side in the Force 5 to 7 gales.

***

Owen Pryce couldn't believe his luck, for months now he'd been out of work, short of money and just about surviving. With his only income from his job-seeker's allowance and busking in the High Street in Holyhead he'd decided to treat himself to a Christmas Eve pint before returning home. He'd lost count of the number of times he'd busked *Stairway to Heaven* that day and sat down in a corner of the pub. There on a window sill next to the table was a mobile phone. He couldn't believe his luck, he thought should he hand it over to the landlord or keep it and maybe get a replacement SIM card for it. In the end when no one was looking he slipped it into his pocket and decided to hang on to it. He then finished his pint, picked up his battered guitar and trudged home to his mother's farmhouse in nearby Penrhos.

***

Friday 25th December, 2015

Greg Henderson was the duty officer on 'A' wing on Christmas morning and he was looking forward to at least getting home to his family to have a late Christmas dinner in the evening. 'Merry Christmas everyone, your breakfast awaits. Come on up you lot, it's a wonderful Christmas morning,' he shouted as he walked down the landing, opening up each of the cells for the day.

The first thing he noticed on the landing as he approached cell A112 was that it had suddenly became cooler, in fact there was a definite chill blowing through from somewhere. He opened the cell door and was staggered to see the broken glass and the bars wrenched apart. He re-locked the cell and dashed back to the duty desk where he rang the alarm bell and called security.

***

'Jim, it's DCI Bentley, I'm sorry to disturb you on Christmas day but there has been an escape from HMP Dinas Bay, guess what it's our friend Ridgway and his partner Ellis. If you switch the TV news on you'll get an update. It appears they escaped last night. I've been in touch with Gwynedd Valley Police and they have promised to keep us informed of any developments. Can you come into my office this afternoon at 4pm and we can decide on how we best handle this? Oh and by the way, Merry Christmas.'

'Merry Christmas, will do sir, I'll be in later on,' said DS Holdsworth, replacing the receiver.

***

Jack Hodgson couldn't believe his ears when he switched on the radio on Christmas morning. The news that two prisoners had escaped from HMP Dinas Bay would normally have just passed him by but also hearing that it was Ridgway and Ellis sent a bit of a shiver down his spine. Could the DCI have been right all along? He was determined to go back to the caravan after Boxing Day to investigate things further.

In the meantime the excitement and sound of the children opening their presents took priority in the Hodgson household.

***

News of the escape spread like wildfire throughout the prison and certainly brought a talking point to the Christmas lunch in the prison dining halls.

'Who would have thought it?' said Higson, who had only just been released from the segregation unit. 'Posh Boy himself escaping, I didn't think he had it in him. Well he's gone up in my estimation I can tell you.'

'Pity he didn't allow a few of us into his plan, we could be sat in front of a nice log fire in a pub somewhere instead of being in this dump,' replied Brown.

'Our turn will come Brownie, we just have to be patient,' responded Higson, 'anyway what are you moaning about, you've got three meals a day, a bed and a nice warm environment. And I'll be round later with the Christmas presents, you will be pleased to know that Father Christmas has made a delivery just before Christmas. He came in his helicopter apparently!'

They all fell about laughing at Higson's remarks.

'Still I'll tell you this, I wouldn't mind betting Posh Boy and his mate are sitting in front of a nice log fire somewhere,' remarked Brown.

In actual fact Ridgway and Ellis at that point were still huddled together shivering in the fishing boat in the middle of the Irish Sea.

***

At three pm, just sixteen hours later, tired, exhausted and extremely sea sick they landed on the beach at Bray, just south of Dun Laoghaire in the Republic of Ireland, where Alan from the Jelly Bean was waiting to greet them on the shoreline.

'And a Merry Christmas to the both of you, did you have a good journey?' he exclaimed.

'That was rough I can tell you Alan, I'm just so glad to get on dry land,' replied Tim, who was still feeling very ill.

'I think I'm going to be sick again,' said Charlie, who by now was very pale as he threw up onto the beach.

Alan paid off the crew in cash for the hire of the boat and they were soon off again out of sight.

'We'll soon get you both sorted out,' he said. 'Now look, I've arranged for you to stay at a nice secluded farmhouse in the Wicklow mountains, you need to lie low for a few days as the news of your escape is already on the TV and radio over here. I did what you said Tim, I left your old mobile phone switched on in a pub in Holyhead, it's fully charged.'

'Great, have you got everything else that we need?'

'Yes, I've retrieved some of the cloned credit cards that you had hidden away plus a forged passport relating to one of the cards as you requested. Oh and there's a new mobile phone topped up and ready to go. Everything is in this rucksack of yours, Tim, together with a change of clothes for both of you. We should be back at the farmhouse in about fifty minutes. We've got the place to ourselves, you can dry yourselves off, we'll soon have you sorted out.'

'Did you manage to organise some cash for us?' asked Tim.

'Yes, no problem, I've got you £750 and 500 euros in cash which should be enough to keep you going for the time being.'

'You are a star, Alan, we really owe you one.'

'Well you've helped me enough times, it's the least I can do for you. Now come on, we need to move fast, the hire car is over there.'

'Can I give you this Alan, but please don't switch it on until you are back in Manchester, leave it on for say an hour and switch it off again,' said Tim, as he handed the mobile phone to him.

**

DS Holdsworth arrived to see DCI Bentley already in his office. He was on the phone to Gwynedd Valley Police when he knocked on the office door. The DCI beckoned him to come in and sit down while he finished the call; eventually he came off the phone.

'Sorry I've had to drag you in to work on Christmas day Jim, but we need to act fast on this, can you please set up the incident room. We've agreed that as we have considerably more information and intelligence on Ridgway and Ellis we will work with Gwynedd Valley Police in trying to find them. I've also agreed that we will lead on the investigation into how they escaped in the first place,' said DCI Bentley. 'Our belief is that Ridgway and Ellis are still in the North Wales area unless of course someone has assisted them with the breakout. On the plus side there would of course only have been limited public transport, there would be no trains or buses on Christmas Eve or today for that matter. Can you and Jean pull together everything we have on Ridgway and Ellis, particularly phone numbers, phone logs, email addresses, financial checks, bank accounts etc., you know the sort of thing, and at least we can follow their trail. I don't like to say I told you so but as you know I had my suspicions about Ridgway all along. Also pull in any additional resources you need to work with you.'

'Yes sir, I'll get in touch with Jean straight away and see what we have on them,' replied DS Holdsworth.

***

Tim, Charlie and Alan had spent the remainder of Christmas day in the old stone farmhouse. Alan had brought in a number of frozen meals together with a few bottles of wine. They sat around a roaring log fire and chatted until the early hours.

'Thanks again for helping us with this, we couldn't have done it without you, Alan,' said Tim, as he tucked into a late Christmas dinner.

'So, what's your plan after this then, Tim? You know you are going to have to be very careful as your photos are likely to be in every newspaper and on TV. You can stay here as long as you like, it belongs to an old friend of mine who plans to put the place up for sale next year.'

'Well at the moment I think we'll stay here until the New Year and then decide on our next move, I hadn't really worked out the next stage to be perfectly honest.'

'When are you planning to return to Manchester, Alan?' enquired Charlie. 'Presumably you will have to get back to the café soon.'

'Well, I have a flight booked from Dublin to Manchester on the 27th, as you say I do need to get back. I'll make sure you have enough provisions here for the week before I go. In the meantime relax and just enjoy your freedom.'

CHAPTER 26

Saturday 26th December, 2015

DS Holdsworth had called in Jean Price and DC Heath to attend the meeting with DCI Bentley. Jean had pulled together everything they had on both individuals and they were now briefing the DCI, who was not in the best of moods, on the information they had gained so far and the possible next moves in tracing Ridgway and Ellis.

DS Holdsworth switched on the laptop projector and opened up the meeting. He waited a short while for his presentation to become available.

'Right, we are now in business. Well sir, Jean has been busy overnight and you can see that we have considerable information on Ridgway already; in particular including his two mobile numbers that he was using prior to his arrest. We suggest that we firstly follow up those mobiles using cell site analysis, at least this will give us a location to within a hundred metres. We have had a quick look already and in the past five minutes we noticed one of the phones is switched off but the other is currently located in a village on the island of Anglesey. We have passed that information onto Gwynedd Valley Police who as we speak are moving into the village. They are being assisted by one of the leading telecommunication surveillance companies so we should hear something very soon. As soon as we have a rough idea of location we can start tracking any CCTV footage in that area. Clearly we can't do this until we have pinned them down to a specific location.'

'Splendid, what about the bank cards, they will clearly need money, they won't be able to last for very long without cash.'

'Yes, we are monitoring each of their bank accounts including any attempts at withdrawing cash from any of the ATMs.'

'Great, hopefully that pair will be back in prison before we know it, but we still don't know what they are planning grand style.'

'I wouldn't bank on them being back in prison, sir, Ridgway is a slippery sort of character.'

***

Owen Pryce was making himself some breakfast when there came a knock on the door. His mother went to answer it and he could hear voices in the hallway.

'Sorry to trouble you madam, we are from Gwynedd Valley Police and we just need to ask you a few questions. May we come in please?' said the police officer.

'Yes of course officer, is there something the matter?'

The two police officers remained silent as they followed Mrs Pryce into the kitchen.

'This is my son, Owen. Owen, these two police officers need to ask us a few questions.'

'Good morning, do either of you know anyone by the name of Tim Ridgway or Charlie Ellis?'

'Tim who, Charlie who?' said Mrs Pryce. 'I've never heard of either of them, what's all this about? There is only my son and myself living here. Do you know anyone of that name, Owen?'

Owen shrugged and continued to butter his toast.

'Well, do you have a mobile phone?'

'Yes, I've got one, it's here,' said Mrs Pryce, handing the phone over.

The officer took a look at it and nodded across to the other officer.

At this point the other officer rang the number he had written down in his notebook and immediately the mobile that Owen had in his pocket rang.

'Can you please answer that, sir?'

Owen picked up his phone and answered it.

'And where exactly did you get this phone sir?

'I found it on a window sill, in the Red Lion public house in Holyhead, officer. It was on Christmas Eve. After Christmas I was going to hand it in,' said Owen, who was now panicking and trying to think quickly. 'I haven't used it, I don't even know what number it is. I wasn't going to keep it, honest.'

'I see, well I will need to take this and give you a receipt for it sir, but we believe this belongs to an escaped prisoner from HMP Dinas Bay. At what time did you find this in the pub, sir?' said the officer, making notes.

'It would be about 9.30pm, officer, I stopped for a quick drink, saw it there and then made my way home.'

'Would you mind if we have a quick look around the house, Mrs Pryce?'

'No please carry on, officer, we don't have anything to hide.'

The two police officers took a look upstairs and in every room and five minutes later came back into the kitchen.'

'Ok, thank you Mrs Pryce, we are sorry to have troubled you.'

***

'They've got Ridgway's old mobile phone sir, it's been found on Anglesey,' said DS Holdsworth as he came off the phone to Gwynedd Valley Police.

'That's great, at least we know roughly where they are,' replied the DCI.

'Well not exactly, sir, the phone was found in a Holyhead pub at 9.30pm on Christmas Eve. It would have been impossible for them to get from Dinas Bay to Holyhead in that time unless they had broken out earlier in the day. No, I'm afraid this has been a plant to try and throw us off the scent. They must have had someone working on the outside to assist them.'

'It could be a double bluff of course, knowing Ridgway, and maybe they are still in fact in the area,' replied the DCI thoughtfully.

'Well it's possible but I doubt it sir, I don't think we are any further on. The other mobile phone which belongs to Ridgway hasn't been switched on as yet but we will keep monitoring that one.'

'I presume Gwynedd Valley Police have alerted all ports, stations and airports?'

'Yes, no problem there, we will be informed if they have any sightings.'

***

'Hi Jean, it's Jack Hodgson. I'm really sorry to trouble you on Boxing Day but I need to have a quick chat if I may.'

'Hello Jack, it's good to hear from you and Merry Christmas, but I'm not sure we should be speaking, as you are still on suspension aren't you?'

'Merry Christmas Jean, well yes I am but I needed to pick your brains on something. I presume you have seen the news that Ridgway and Ellis have escaped and I assume you are still assigned to the investigation?' enquired Jack.

'Yes, in fact we are working with North Wales on investigating it. The DCI is still convinced that these are the prisoners we should be focussing on. I'm still personally not convinced myself,' said Jean.

'No, as you know I agree, I think this is just a diversion of something much bigger. I have been studying my notes and I think some kind of smuggling is going on there. I don't have any details but I intend to go back to the caravan and see what I can uncover. I'm not sure I mentioned it but whilst I was out walking along the cliffs a few weeks ago not far from the prison, I saw something suspicious with boxes being unloaded from a small boat. It was a man and a woman who loaded them into a 4x4 and I tried to hear what they were discussing but I couldn't get too close. I managed to pick out two words in their conversation which seemed to be repeated a few times, I think it was the name "*Gwen*" and "*unease*" which doesn't mean anything to me. Does the name mean anything to you? I was wondering if the name Gwen had cropped up as part of your data collation and analysis?'

'Strange, it doesn't mean anything to me either, I don't know who she is, we have no one of that name recorded.'

'Anyway, I intend to go back and see what I can find, keep it to yourself, I don't want Bentley or anyone else to hear about this, otherwise I'll be in even more trouble than I'm already in. I'll be in touch but if you hear anything then let me know, bye for now.'

CHAPTER 27

Sunday 27th December, 2015

Alan bade farewell to Tim and Charlie and he drove straight to Dublin airport. He handed back the hire car and checked in at the terminal, allowing plenty of time for the Easy Jet flight to Manchester. He couldn't help noticing the extra police presence at the airport that presumably was on the lookout for Tim and Charlie.

He boarded the flight which was only half full, which part way through the Christmas period was not really surprising. He settled down to read the newspaper which was now full of the news of the prison escape and the fraud crimes that had led to their convictions. The short flight to Manchester was on time and as he made his way into the airport terminal building at Terminal 1 he switched the mobile phone on that Tim had given him. By the time he had reached the Jelly Bean café he had switched the phone off again as arranged.

***

Sue Hodgson was not impressed when Jack said he had to return to North Wales but this time at least he promised to return home in a few days. He packed his bag, loaded up the Volvo estate and set off for the caravan. He had decided to dispense with switching cars; after all he had no intention whatsoever of going anywhere near the prison. He decided however he would still need to maintain his undercover identity for the time being at least. The traffic was lighter than usual and three hours later he arrived at the caravan site. The caravan was dreadfully cold and he switched on the gas fire and opened the bedroom and bathroom doors to warm the whole place up. He made himself a spot of lunch and he was just about to start working out a plan of action when his mobile rang.

'Hello Jack, its Jean. I've had a thought on what those two people were saying, remember the ones you saw on the beach. Did you say they were unloading boxes from a small boat?'

'Hi, Jean, yes I couldn't hear them very well, the wind was howling a bit at the time.'

'Well, I don't think they were referring to someone called Gwen, I think they could have been speaking Welsh and they were referring to an island off the peninsula about five miles out. If you have access to a local map you will see the island is called Ynys Gwyn; it means the White Island. It originally housed a monastery in the 12th century which lasted until the dissolution of the monasteries in 1536. I looked it up, it's now a bird sanctuary just off the Welsh coast. Apparently it's now home to many seabirds and in particular a colony of cormorants.'

'That's amazing Jean, it could have been that place they were referring to, maybe I should take a look at this island of Ynys Gwyn. Whatever they were bringing in I feel sure it has some sort of a connection with this place.'

'Just a thought Jack, do you think you might find Ridgway and Ellis holed up there?'

'Well, that's a distinct possibility as well and it's definitely worth checking out but my guess is they are long gone from the area. Thanks Jean, not a word about this to anyone, understood?'

Jean smiled. 'Understood, Jack, my lips are sealed, I'll speak to you soon.'

***

DCI Bentley was briefing the investigation team on the latest developments in the incident room at Midshire Police HQ. They had been joined by DS Colin Jones from Gwynedd Valley Police who had been seconded to the team as the main liaison officer to work alongside them.

'Once again sorry for disturbing your Christmas plans, with a bit of luck we can hopefully bring this investigation to a close and capture the escaped prisoners,' said the DCI. 'Now as I mentioned before the investigation falls into three strands, which are of course all closely connected. Firstly the investigation into how the break-out from the prison actually occurred; clearly Ridgway and Ellis have had assistance from outside and we need to get to the bottom of this, we need to find out who it was that has actually been helping them. Secondly we need to track them down and put them back where they belong, behind bars. Finally we are led to believe that this is part of a much grander scheme involving a network of external contacts, we need to know what it is they are planning. All three strands will be investigated as part of Operation Predator, a joint investigation between Midshire and Gwynedd Valley Police.'

'DS Colin Jones and DC Heath will take charge of the first strand – the breakout. We need to know who has helped them with this escape. They clearly could not have done this on their own. I suggest you start by looking at who their visitors have been since they first entered the prison. We also need to know who they have been calling from the PIN phones on the prison wing. DS Holdsworth will work with me on tracking Ridgway and Ellis down. For the time being we will hold fire on the final strand unless further information comes into play of course. Jean, I would like you to work across all the lines of enquiry and assist the team with any indexing, research and analysis.'

***

'Good afternoon, it's good to see you again John, and Merry Christmas to you. I didn't recognise you at first, I see the beard has gone, it has taken years off you. Now what can I get you?' said Steve, the landlord at the Smithy Arms.

'Yeah, I decided to ditch the beard, it was getting a bit itchy to be honest. I'll have a pint of your best bitter please, Steve,' replied Jack Hodgson, who had decided he had to maintain the John Hughes identity whilst he was in North Wales. 'Tell me, I don't suppose you know anyone who would hire a small fishing boat, just for the day?'

'I do indeed, my brother-in-law Andy has a small fishing boat and he can help you with that, mind you he would need to come with you of course. If you give me your details I'll get him to call you. He keeps it on the quayside at Trefor, it's a twenty-three footer but is kitted out with all the right equipment. I've been out on it myself with him, a great little boat. I'm sure he wouldn't charge you much for it, it would give him an excuse to take it out.'

'Yes, that would be great Steve, ask him to ring me on this number?' replied Jack enthusiastically, handing over a piece of paper across the bar.

'So you fancy a spot of winter fishing, then?' asked Steve.

John laughed. 'No, not exactly, I fancy visiting Ynys Gwyn.'

Steve the landlord looked somewhat shocked.

'Did you say Ynys Gwyn?'

'Yes, why?' replied John, who was puzzled at Steve's response.

'Oh, nothing it's just not the sort of place I would recommend visiting this time of year.'

CHAPTER 28

Monday 28th December, 2015

'I'm getting bored here Tim, when can we make a move? We are stuck in the middle of nowhere and it's going to be difficult getting provisions without any transport,' enquired Charlie, who was struggling to get used to life on the run.

'I know the feeling Charlie, I'm beginning to think we should make a move further north. The public transport has started up again and I think it would be good if we could get into Scotland for the New Year. What do you think?'

'It sounds good to me, Tim. I'd like to move on as soon as possible.'

'Right, well first thing in the morning we'll head down to Wicklow town, from there we should be able to catch a local train into Dublin and then head up towards Belfast. I think we will however need to keep out of the cities wherever possible. We should be able to find a quiet B&B on the way. Somewhere out in the sticks, away from CCTV and the like.'

'Great but we can't stay on the run forever, Tim, we do need a long term plan of action.'

'I agree. Well I've got an uncle who lives in Scotland, we will be fine there for a while, I am sure he can bring us provisions. If we head up to Larne we can get a ferry over to Cairnryan. Longer term I think I need to get out of the UK. How do you feel about eventually going over to France or even further afield? At least maybe there we can start rebuilding our lives under a fresh identity.'

'Suits me, I think I just want to get as far away as possible. There's nothing for me back home.'

'Cheer up, Charlie, we'll head off at first light in the morning.'

***

DS Colin Jones and DC Heath had travelled over to HMP Dinas Bay to have a meeting with the Head of Security to discuss in detail how Ridgway and Ellis had escaped.

'Good morning sir, thank you for agreeing to this meeting so quickly,' said DS Jones as he shook hands with Tom Fletcher.

'Not at all, it's Tom by the way, please call me Tom.'

'Oh, right, I'm Colin and this is Clive, we do appreciate your time.'

'It is no problem at all Colin, as I was saying to you on the phone yesterday, we are keen to clear this up as fast as possible and learn from any mistakes that may have been made here. The governor as you can imagine is highly embarrassed about the situation, particularly when you consider how new the prison itself is. As you know this is the first escape this prison has encountered.'

'Can you firstly tell us how you believe Ridgway and Ellis made their escape without being spotted or setting off any alarm?'

'Yes, certainly, it's still a bit of a mystery to us to be honest. I can show you best on this aerial photograph of the prison.'

The three men walked over to the far wall where a large framed aerial photograph of the prison was on display.

'This is their cell here, which overlooks the rooftop, and to the right you can see the exercise yard, beyond that and in the distance is the sea. Ridgway and Ellis would somehow firstly have had to gain access to two ultra-high quality hacksaw blades, which they used to saw through the prison bars. We found these discarded under the bottom bunk bed. It must have taken them absolutely ages to saw through them. They then smashed what we believed to be toughened glass which shattered once it had been hit hard several times. They then crept out and we think they made their way across the roof top to the first CCTV camera position. Now somehow this hasn't picked them up, we don't know why, and we are calling in the company that installed them to check everything out. From here they must have gone along the exercise yard wall, somehow cut through the razor wire and dropped over the side to the rocks below. It's a wonder they haven't injured themselves to be honest. Again they would have somehow bypassed a second CCTV camera.'

'I don't know if you are aware, Tom,' interrupted DC Heath, 'but Ridgway is highly skilled in Information Technology and could well have tinkered with your network connecting these cameras.'

'No, I wasn't aware of that, thank you for informing me. To be honest we don't normally assess the skill profiles of each prisoner here so maybe that's another lesson we need to learn from.'

'Did you find anything else in the cell, anything out of the norm?' quizzed DC Heath.

'Well we did find this old bible, but prisoners often turn to the bible, it gives them comfort,' replied Tom Fletcher, reaching into his drawer.

'Can I see that?' asked DC Heath.

'Yes, certainly,' replied Tom Fletcher, handing it over.

'Well I may be wrong but I think this is how the hacksaw blades had been smuggled in. You can see the stitching has come loose and is a different thread on the spine.'

'Fascinating, I hadn't even spotted that.'

'How many prison officers would have been on duty, Tom?' enquired DS Jones.

'Well, we have been short staffed somewhat but on Christmas Eve we would have had our normal levels. I can't give you an exact figure and I would have to check that.'

'One of the things we are interested in, Tom, are the visitor records; do you have those so we can have a quick look?'

'Yes, most definitely, I thought you would want to see those, here they are. We keep them electronically,' said Tom, as he swung the computer screen round. 'If we firstly search on Ridgway's visitors you can see that he has had visits from Father O'Brien and a Mr Alan Smith. If we now search on Charlie Ellis's visit records you can see that he hasn't received any, which is unusual.'

'Now looking at this in a bit more detail you can see that Father O'Brien has been to the prison twice and this guy Alan Smith from the Jelly Bean café has attended once.'

'Interesting,' said DS Jones, 'looking at the addresses both of these visitors live over in Manchester so I suggest we head back there and arrange an interview with each of them. Oh, I almost forgot, could you let us have the PIN phone call logs relating to any phone calls made by Ridgway and Ellis?'

'Yes, I thought you would want those, I've already printed those off for you,' replied Tom Fletcher, as he handed over a printout.

'Well thank you Tom, you have been most helpful, we will get back to you in due course.'

'Anytime Colin and Clive, it's good to meet you.'

***

'Is that John Hughes?' said the voice on the other end of the telephone.

'Yes, it is, who am I speaking to?'

'My name is Andy Brown. I've been given your number by my brother-in-law Steve at the Smithy Arms. I understand you want to hire a boat for the day, is that right?'

'Yes, thanks for calling Andy, I need to get out to Ynys Gwyn, is that something you can help me with?'

'I thought you wanted to hire the boat as soon as possible. I presume you want to visit the island in the summer?'

'I really need to get out there this week.'

There was an audible sharp intake of breath down the telephone.

'I wouldn't recommend going there at this time of year John, the weather can be atrocious and there are very few places to land on the island. Can it not wait until the weather improves a little?'

'No, I'm afraid not Andy, so are you prepared to take me out there?'

'Well, yes I can take you out there but it will cost you.'

'How much would you want?'

'I think we are looking at £150 for the day, all in.'

'Ok, it's a deal, how about tomorrow?' replied John Hughes, wondering how on earth he was going to claim that back from Midshire Police when he wasn't even supposed to be there.

'Tomorrow is fine, meet me down at the harbour at Trefor, I'll be there on the boat at 10.00am.'

'Great, hang on, what's the boat called?'

'Oh right, yes you can't miss it, it's called *"Miss Behavin"*.'

***

Tuesday 29th December, 2015

Tim Ridgway and Charlie Ellis were up very early. They tidied the farmhouse up as best they could, locked the door, placed the key as arranged under a large stone flowerpot and started walking down through the country lanes to Wicklow. The day was still very young and an early morning winter mist lay sprawled across the surrounding fields. They had only been walking about two miles when a farm tractor and trailer pulled up alongside them.

'Top of the morning to you boys, a grand day it is, now you must be lost around these parts?' said the tractor driver.

'I don't suppose you are going anywhere near Wicklow?' enquired Tim, who had already started tiring.

'I am indeed, hop into the trailer and I'll soon get you there, sure that will be no problem at all,' came the reply.

They climbed into the trailer which looked as though it hadn't been cleaned ever since it was new and over the years must have transported everything from livestock to manure. Eventually after half an hour they arrived at the delightful town of Wicklow.

'Well, this is as far as we go now lads, unless that is you want to help me buy a few animals from the market.'

'Erm, no thanks, but we really appreciated the ride though,' said Charlie as he cleaned off his trousers.

'Ah grand, it's no trouble lads, you have a good day.'

Tim and Charlie then made their way to the railway station and ten minutes later they were heading on the 09.04 train to Dublin.

***

DS Jones and DC Heath had returned to Midshire Police HQ. They had passed on the phone log from the wing PINS system to Jean Price, who was downloading it into the link analysis software. They were now in the process of contacting Father O'Brien from the information they had noted from the visitor records.

'Hello, is that Father O'Brien?' said DS Jones.

'It is, yes and who might I be speaking to?'

'My name is Detective Sergeant Jones from Gwynedd Valley Police, I wonder if you are available for a short interview this afternoon.'

'Yes, I'm free this afternoon but can you please tell me what this is about, I haven't been speeding again have I?'

'No, it's nothing like that. I understand you visited Timothy Ridgway at HMP Dinas Bay.'

'That's correct, is Tim ok, he's not had an accident or anything?'

'Well no, Father O'Brien, Tim Ridgway has escaped from prison.'

'He's done what! Oh, dear I am sorry to hear about that, yes I'm free after 2pm, I'll be glad to be of any assistance.'

'DC Heath and I will call and see you at 2pm. Goodbye for now.'

***

John Hughes glanced at his watch, it was 9.45 a.m. and he was running late, having overslept. He'd rushed through his breakfast and prayed he would get there in time and be down at the quayside to meet Andy Brown.

He stepped on the accelerator and shot down the winding country lanes and eventually arrived at the Trefor village car park at 10.15. He rushed over to the harbour and sure enough there it was, moored directly at the quayside, the *"Miss Behavin."* The vessel was smaller than he had first imagined and as he got nearer he could see a tall bearded man on deck in his fifties checking ropes and getting the boat ready for departure.

'You must be Andy, I guess, sorry I'm a bit late, I had one too many nightcaps last night.'

'Ah, we are all ready for you, no problem John, come on board, it's good to meet you.'

John stepped on board, shook hands and settled down inside the small cabin.

'A neat little boat, Andy, how long have you had it?' enquired John, looking around, 'in great condition although I must admit I know nothing whatsoever about boating.'

'It's a her John, about three years now, I bought it off a bloke who could no longer afford to run it with mooring fees and the like. I use her more now for fishing trips. She's a nice little earner in the summer. Just give me a few minutes and we'll be off.'

'No problem, I'm ready when you are,' replied John Hughes.

Some ten minutes later Andy steered the little boat out of the harbour and they headed off into the open seas.

'How long will it take us, Andy?'

'Depends on the weather conditions, it's fine at present and we are not expecting any rough seas. I would guess we should be there in just over an hour, all being well.'

***

The train pulled into Dublin Connolly station exactly on schedule at 10.15am. Tim and Charlie alighted and agreed to separate to avoid being seen together. Each in turn walked over and obtained their ticket for the next part of the journey from the automatic ticket machine and then made their way across to platform one in readiness for the Belfast train. They had previously decided to keep out of the city centre to avoid as many CCTV cameras as possible. In forty-five minutes time as planned, they would be heading north for the town of Lurgan in Northern Ireland.

***

'Thank you for agreeing to meet us at such short notice, Father,' said DS Jones, as he flashed his warrant card, 'now can you tell us the purpose of your visit to see Timothy Ridgway?'

'Well, Tim had requested that I go over to see him. I had been a friend of his family for a number of years and it was the least I could do when I heard he was in prison. I don't know whether you know but Tim lost his parents at an early age in a very bad car crash. It took him a long time to get over it, in fact when I think about it, he never really did get over it, which is part of his problem today. As I say he asked to see me.'

'How did he contact you, did he write to you or ring you up?' enquired DC Heath.

'No, a friend of his contacted me by phone and apparently Tim had asked him to call me.'

'Can you remember the name of this person who called you?' asked DS Jones.

'I think it was Alan something, do you know I can't remember his surname, it's an age thing you know. Alan erm, it will come to me.'

'Was it Alan Smith by any chance?' asked DC Heath, looking up from his notebook.

'Yes, that was it, Alan Smith, I never actually met him but yes he said Tim had been asking to see me as soon as possible.'

'So was there any particular reason that you went back there a couple of weeks later?' asked DS Jones.

'Pardon? I didn't go back there, I have only attended the prison once. You must be mistaken.'

'Well according to the prison's records Father, you have had two visits there, once on the 21st November and a week later on the 28th November,' interjected DC Heath, who looked up from making his notes.

'No, I only went there once, I assure you. Let me get my diary and I'll confirm the date.'

Father O'Brien limped over to the bookshelf and located a red diary.

'Let me see now, yes, here we are on Saturday, the 21st November. I had stayed with my sister and her family on the previous night and she drove me over there from her house at Menai Bridge. On the 28thNovember I had lunch in Manchester with Bishop O'Reilly at his house.'

'Are you absolutely sure about that Father, as HMP Dinas Bay has a record of you visiting there on the 28th at 2pm?'

'I'm absolutely sure, you can ask the Bishop, we had quite a long lunch and I'm sure you will agree that there is no way I could be in two places at the same time.'

'Did Tim Ridgway ask you to bring anything in for him?' enquired DS Jones, who was clearly mystified at this information.

'No, I don't think so. Oh yes, sorry, he asked me to send him a bible. Do you know I've completely forgotten all about that? I never did get round to that, I remember asking one of the officers on duty would it be ok for me to send him in a bible. He said it would be fine. It's completely slipped my mind and I suppose it's a bit late now.'

'Just a little bit Father,' said DC Heath.

***

The little fishing boat was struggling to make progress in the Force 5 headwind and John Hughes was now feeling decidedly ill.

'How much further Andy?' asked John, 'I'm trying my best to keep my breakfast down.'

'Not far now John, in fact you can see the island coming into view on the starboard side of the boat, just over there,' pointed Andy.

John looked over to the right hand side of the boat and sure enough there in the distance now coming into view was Ynys Gwyn, looming out of the fog. The little boat turned and Andy skilfully steered it out of the wind towards a small jetty just big enough to take a single craft. Ten minutes later they were alongside and Andy tied the boat up to a rusting Samson post.

'Well I'll stay back here with the boat and let you explore if that's ok with you,' said Andy, 'unless you need help of course. Go carefully on the jetty as it's very slippery. I'll make us a spot of lunch for when you get back.'

'That sounds good Andy, I shouldn't be too long,' replied John as he stepped out and made his way up the carved out stone steps into a thick wooded area. As he clambered upwards through the woods he could hear the seabirds high above him, hundreds of them, almost telling him that he was invading their island. Eventually his path cleared into a large opening and there it was before him, in a commanding position overlooking the island, the remains of the monastery. It was a grey stone building which had long fallen into disrepair, now covered in trees and bushes. He walked around the side looking for some sort of opening to the building, a doorway or a window, and there almost out of a view at the rear was a large oak door. It was padlocked but the padlock was new, very new in fact. He couldn't see into the building but he could see footprints in the mud on the path. He decided that he should make his way back to the boat but there was no doubt the old monastery was definitely being used to store something, and it certainly wasn't food for the birds.

***

Sisters Janet and Pauline McQuillan were sitting at home in front of the fire, knitting and watching daytime television, when the doorbell rang that afternoon.

'I wonder who on earth that can be?' Janet said, 'are you expecting anyone, Pauline?'

'I've no idea, I'm certainly not expecting anyone.'

Janet made her way through to the hallway and opened the door, keeping it on the chain. She peered around the door.

'Yes, can I help you?'

'Oh, we are sorry to trouble you miss, but do you have a twin room for the night? It's just that we saw the B&B sign at the end of the driveway,' asked Tim Ridgway.

'Well yes, we don't normally have guests in the winter but I'm sure we can accommodate you, come in,' she replied, as she unfastened the chain.

'Who is it, Janet?' came the shout from the lounge.

'We have two guests!' Janet shouted back. 'Now gentlemen if you'd please sign the visitors' book and I'll get you the key to room two, which has twin beds. It will be £40 per night. I assume you are alright with that?'

'Yes, no problem, that will be fine,' replied Tim, handing over two twenty pound notes.

'Would you like to go and fetch your bags from the car?'

'Oh, we don't have any, it's all in this rucksack.'

'Really, travelling light, oh well, you'll find everything you need upstairs, your room is on the first floor and breakfast will be served from 7 o'clock. Just give me a shout if you need anything.'

'Great, thank you, erm, Mrs…?'

'You can call me Janet.'

Tim and Charlie made their way upstairs and Janet returned to continue her knitting in the lounge.

'Two nice young men, Pauline, although I'm sure I've seen them before somewhere, ah well, it's good to have visitors out of season.'

CHAPTER 29

Wednesday 30th December, 2015

'Are you sure he is telling you the truth?' demanded DCI
Bentley, 'I mean the prison has a record of him visiting
on a second occasion.'

'Well I don't know what to believe anymore,'
replied DS Jones, 'we've asked the prison to check
through CCTV footage of the visitors on the 28th
November. They have confirmed that someone meeting
the description of Father O'Brien definitely came to visit
Tim Ridgway and what's more handed over a bible to
him in front of the prison officers on duty. It seems to
have slipped his mind that he'd handed over a bible.
When we spoke to the prison officers who were on duty
in the visitors' waiting room they distinctly remember
him coming in, he has a noticeable limp, something he
acquired through a motorbike accident apparently.'

'I think we have to invite Father O'Brien in for a
further interview. I'm not at all happy with the situation,

I think he could be hiding something, get him in here now,' replied the DCI, 'and have you got anywhere with the other visitor?'

'His name is Alan Smith,' responded DC Heath.

'Well clearly we have to trace this Alan Smith whoever he is, what do we know about him?' asked the DCI.

'Well he is next on our list sir, he owns and runs the Jelly Bean café in Manchester, we are going there this afternoon,' said DS Jones.

'Did you say the Jelly Bean?' asked DS Holdsworth, who had suddenly sat up.

'Yes, why do you know him? What's so special about the Jelly Bean cafe?'

'We certainly do know him and it was his café where we made some of the arrests on the original fraud identity theft cases. I should have thought about that connection, yes we suspected Alan Smith as being somehow involved in the identity theft cases at the time, but never pursued it.'

'Well, I suggest you get round there straight away after our meeting, DS Jones, and find out all you can about our Mr Smith,' demanded the DCI.

'Now moving on to where we are with tracking Ridgway and Ellis. We have had no sightings to report on Anglesey and the mobile phone was clearly there to throw us off the scent. All railway and bus stations are being monitored but again there are no reported sightings. So at this stage I can only think that they are holed up somewhere in North Wales.'

'Excuse me sir, but do you think it's possible that they are now in Ireland?' questioned DS Jones.

'Well, I suppose it's possible, although I'm not sure they would have had the support to get over there. We have checked CCTV footage from Holyhead and there is no way they left through that port, although we have informed the Garda Siochana and the PSNI as a precaution,' responded the DCI.

'Jean, do we have anything yet on the bank accounts of Ridgway and Ellis?'

'No, nothing at all sir, we are monitoring them but there haven't been any withdrawals made since they first entered prison.'

'They must be getting money from somewhere or someone. Someone is definitely helping them. In the meantime DS Holdsworth and I will be visiting this Father O'Brien character to arrest him on suspicion of assisting with a prison escape.'

***

The smell of a wonderful Ulster fry full breakfast wafting up the stairs had lured Tim and Charlie downstairs to the dining room. They sat down and tucked into an enormous breakfast of two fried eggs, the all-important lightly browned potato and soda bread, pork sausages, rashers of crispy bacon, black and white pudding, brown sauce and a large juicy red tomato– truly a great start to any day.

'So, where are you gentlemen off to next?' said Janet. 'Presumably you'll be wanting to celebrate New Year's Eve, somewhere nice on your travels?'

'Probably in Dublin,' said Tim, lying, who clearly didn't wish to leave a trail.

'Well, I'm sure you'll enjoy the city,' said Janet, 'now if there is anything else you need just give Pauline or me a shout. We will be in the kitchen.'

'We should be fine thank you, we will be off straight after breakfast but thank you ever so much for your hospitality, it was just what we needed.'

Janet joined Pauline in the kitchen and left the two of them to enjoy their breakfast in peace, but she was still sure that before they had turned up yesterday she had seen them somewhere else.

***

John Hughes decided he'd had more than enough sailing for the time being and was so glad to be back on dry land. The journey back from Ynys Gwyn to the harbour the previous day had been horrendous and he had been violently ill on the stern of Andy's boat. He had decided to return home to celebrate New Year with his family. Everything else would have to wait for now. There was no doubt about it, something was going on and it involved that island and he had to get to the bottom of it. But try as he might he couldn't get it out of his mind. The traffic on the way home was busier than normal with shoppers out for post-Christmas sale bargains and whilst sitting in a lengthy traffic queue outside Chester he suddenly had a thought as to his next move. He called up the number on his hands free mobile.

'Pete, it's Jack Hodgson, how are you? It's a long time no speak.'

'Hi Jack, it's good to hear from you, is the rumour right that you've been suspended by old Bentley?'

'Afraid so Pete, I can't explain it now but I disagreed with him too many times. Look, I need a favour.'

'Of course, what is it?'

'Well remember when you were seconded to the National Crime Agency not so long ago, do you have a contact there that I could talk to? It needs to be someone who covers the North Wales region and someone I can trust.'

'Yes of course, DC Bryn Lewis is worth talking to, I'm pretty sure he's still assigned to the NCA. He's a top guy, you'll get on well with him. I'll text you his number and I'll ring him and tell him to expect your call.'

'Great, thanks Pete and not a word about this to anyone.'

***

Police continuing to search for two Manchester men who escaped from HMP Dinas Bay in North Wales have arrested a 63-year-old priest on suspicion of assisting offenders in a daring prison escape on Christmas Eve.

Timothy John Ridgway, aged 26, and Charles Ellis, 25, from Manchester, were reported to Midshire Police after they escaped from HMP Dinas Bay, near Caernarvon on Christmas Eve, December 24th. Both Gwynedd Valley Police and Midshire Police are investigating the dramatic escape.

Police believe that both men may still be in the North Wales area and enquiries are ongoing to locate and arrest them.

Head of Serious Crime at Midshire Police – Detective Superintendent Pomeroy said:

"We think the two men are more than likely to be still in North Wales or may possibly have returned to Manchester. We have officers in both these areas who are tasked with searching and arresting them. Both of them were serving sentences for fraud and identity theft and whilst there is nothing to suggest they are any risk to the public we would still ask people not to approach them and to ring either Midshire or Gwynedd Valley Police as a matter of urgency with any information."

**

Tim and Charlie said farewell to Janet and Pauline and made their way down the road to the old but modernised railway station at Lurgan. They bought tickets from the machine for Larne changing at Belfast City and didn't have to wait long before the 08.38 Belfast train arrived. They had decided early on that they would sit apart on the train and meet up again when they were at the harbour side at Larne Ferry terminal.

What they hadn't banked on was someone following them to the train station.

**

The Jelly Bean café was busy considering the students were still on holiday. The café was bustling with shoppers stopping in for a coffee break and resting their weary feet. Alan Smith was busy serving a customer when the two police officers came in.

'What can I get you?' asked Alan, not even suspecting they were police officers.

'Are you Alan Smith?' asked DS Jones, flashing his ID card.

'Yes, why is there something wrong?'

'May we please have a word with you? Is there somewhere quieter we can talk?'

'Yes, in the back room. Susy, can you please look after everything, I just need to have a chat with these two gentlemen,' said Alan Smith to his assistant.

They went into the back room, which was simply furnished with a table and four chairs and an armchair next to an old fireplace.

'Please sit down gents, so, how can I be of assistance?'

'Did you visit Timothy Ridgway in prison a few weeks ago?' asked DS Jones, looking at his notes.

'Yes, I did, I went to see him not long after he had been taken into HMP Dinas Bay.'

'Were you aware that Tim Ridgway and Charlie Ellis had now escaped from the prison?'

'Yes, I read about it in the national newspapers.'

'Do you know anyone by the name Father O'Brien?'

'Yes, I know of him, I have never met him but I spoke to him on the telephone. Tim had asked me to contact him to ask him whether he could pay him a visit.'

'How many times have you visited Tim Ridgway in prison?'

'I think you'll find I have only visited him once.'

'Has Tim Ridgway been in touch with you throughout his stay in prison?'

'A couple of times, he rang me from the PIN phone on the wing.'

'Has he been in touch with you since his escape?'

'No, I have no idea where he or Charlie are. I just hope they are safe and well. Now if you have no more questions I must get back to the café, as you can see we are very busy.'

'Well that will be all for now, Mr Smith, but we may need to come back and ask you further questions at a later date, thank you for your time.'

The two officers left the café and made their way back to DC Heath's car.

'He's lying of course, his body language said it all,' said DC Heath, 'we certainly need to find out what he's been up to in the past few weeks. I'll get on to Jean to see what she can uncover about our Mr Smith. I wonder how the boss is getting on with interviewing Father O'Brien.'

***

Tim Ridgway and Charlie Ellis had now arrived at Larne ferry terminal. Tim had already booked their tickets online using one of the stolen credit cards that he had been keeping for such an occasion. They boarded the

13.30 European Causeway ship and settled down in the passenger lounge for the two hour ferry crossing to Cairnryan in Scotland.

'How far is it to your uncle's place from Cairnryan, Tim?' said Charlie, forgetting about who could be listening.

'Keep your voice down. About an hour away, I rang him last night and he's agreed to pick us up at the ferry terminal as soon as we dock. I haven't seen him for a while so I just hope he recognises me,' said Tim quietly.

'Well your picture in all the papers should have reminded him!' grinned Charlie.

'Eh, don't laugh Charlie, I'm hoping no one has spotted us yet that's why we really do need to lie low for as long as possible.'

***

'Is that the Police Service of Northern Ireland?'

'It is indeed, how can we help you, madam?' replied the desk sergeant.

'My name is Janet McQuillan. My sister Pauline and I run a guest house in Lurgan. We have some information on the two escaped prisoners.'

'Really madam, and which prisoners would those be?'

'Well how many are there? I read about it in the national newspaper and heard it on the news. Two prisoners have escaped from a prison somewhere in Wales. I think it was on Christmas Eve when they actually escaped and last night I believe they stayed at our bed and breakfast.'

'Right madam, well I'll take your details and pass them on to the relevant department and someone will contact you in due course.'

***

The European Causeway docked at Cairnryan bang on schedule at 15.30. It had been a straightforward and comfortable crossing. Tim and Charlie decided it would be best if on arrival they split up and leave the vessel separately. Charlie sat in the lounge whilst the car/cargo passengers returned to their vehicles and the foot passengers made their way to the disembarkation point. Tim followed the line of passengers out through the terminal building and on to the car park. He didn't have to wait long when the battered Land Rover Defender came squealing round the bend and parked immediately in front him. Tim waved to him, he hadn't seen his uncle for almost ten years but he hadn't changed a bit.

'Well it's good to see you Timothy after all these years and where's this friend of yours?'

'Hi Uncle Bill, yes it's good to see you and you haven't changed a bit.'

'Call me Bill, Tim. Uncle makes me feel really old.'

'Charlie should be coming through in a moment,' replied Tim, 'hang on there he is, give him a flash of your headlights.'

Bill Ridgway flashed the lights on the Land Rover and Charlie came dashing over and climbed into the back.

'Charlie, meet my Uncle Bill. Bill this is Charlie, he's a good friend of mine.'

'Hello Mr Ridgway.'

'Hello Charlie, it's good to meet you, any friend of Tim's is a friend of mine. You can call me Bill. Right let's get off now, we'll soon have you back at my old place and you can stay there as long as you like.'

They had been travelling now for nearly an hour down country lanes and deserted farm tracks.

'How much further is it?' asked Charlie as he was being thrown around the back seat of the Land Rover.

'Not far now,' replied Bill Ridgway, 'sit tight, it does get a little bumpier along this stretch.'

CHAPTER 30

Thursday 31st December, 2015

'Is that DC Bryn Lewis?'

'Yes, it is and who am I speaking to?'

'My name is Jack Hodgson, I'm a DC in Midshire Police and a colleague of mine, Pete Bradbury, who I understand you have worked with, kindly gave me your details.'

'Ah yes, Pete called me to tell me that you would call. How can I help you, Jack?'

'Well Bryn, it's a bit sensitive to discuss it over the phone but I wondered if we could meet up as soon as possible, ideally tomorrow afternoon if you are available?'

'Yes, I will need a bit of time to sober up after tonight's celebrations. Can you come over here to Caernarvon?'

'Yes of course, that's no problem, shall we say 4pm?'

'Yeah that's fine, I suggest my local pub, "The Rose and Thistle", which is only walking distance from my home. We can meet there and use a private room so we shouldn't get disturbed or for that matter overheard. I know the landlord very well. You can't miss the pub, it's just off the main A487, your sat-nav should find it ok. I look forward to meeting you.'

***

DS Jones and DC Heath were in deep discussion with DCI Bentley regarding how their interview had gone with Alan Smith at the Jelly Bean cafe when the DCI's phone rang.

'Good morning sir, my name is Sergeant Walker from Lurgan Police Station in Northern Ireland. I understand that you are in charge of the investigation regarding the two escaped prisoners from HMP Dinas Bay, the names are Ridgway and Ellis?'

'Yes that is correct, how can I help you?'

'Well we have received a phone call to say that they have been sighted in Lurgan yesterday. Apparently they were staying in a bed and breakfast in the town. I have a contact for you, which is Miss Janet McQuillan at Holdbrook Farm, Lurgan. She is the owner of the B&B.'

'That's excellent, Sergeant, we will follow up this up straight away with Janet McQuillan, thank you for your call.'

The DCI noted down the contact details and called DS Holdsworth into the office, who was working nearby.

'Jim, we don't seem to be making any progress with Father O'Brien, he's not telling us anything. I think we have no option but to release him without charge, he seems to have a very good alibi. Now I do have some interesting news, however, I've just taken a call from Northern Ireland. I believe Ridgway and Ellis are there, we have had a possible sighting yesterday, can you get onto it, here are the contact details of the lady who says they apparently stayed at her bed and breakfast.'

'I'll get straight onto to it sir, that does sound promising. I'll ring her now.'

DS Holdsworth returned to his own office with the latest news.

'Jean, our friends are in Ireland apparently!'

'Well, there's a coincidence,' replied Jean, 'I've just been wading through Alan Smith's recent bank transactions and emails, he's just arrived back from a trip to Ireland!'

***

Tim and Charlie had settled into the farmhouse, which was miles from anywhere, deep in the Galloway Forest Park.

'There's only one thing wrong with this place,' said Tim despondently, as he played with his mobile phone.

'What's that?' replied Charlie, who was busy glancing through the vast library in the dining room.

'Well I've just about got a mobile phone signal but there's no internet!'

'You're joking. I mean have you seen this selection of books, it's massive and certainly offering more than the one in the prison. You've got the TV and this is a beautiful location. Surely you can manage without the internet for once,' replied Charlie, rolling his eyes.

'Well I'm going to have to I suppose but I need to keep an eye on whether the police are onto us or not.'

'I can't see how they would follow us here, I'm not sure I could find this place myself even when I know roughly where it is. What on earth made your uncle come and live up here in the first place?'

Just then Bill Ridgway appeared from the kitchen.

'Oh that was easy Charlie, I needed to get away from the city. I'd had a messy divorce, lost my job, had no prospects whatsoever and I needed peace and quiet. I'd always fancied living up here and as you say it is a most beautiful area. You are only on this planet once you know. I've been living here now about eight years, very settled, my pension keeps me going, I have no debts. I stock up once a month down in Stranraer and that's me sorted out.'

'Oh, sorry Bill I didn't mean for you to hear that,' said Charlie apologetically.

'That's fine Charlie, it's not everyone's ideal situation living out here but I love the peace and tranquillity of the place. Oh and by the way I've stocked up for tonight and I've got a few tasty whiskies I'd like you to try.'

'Sounds good to me, I can't wait.'

***

'Is that Mrs Janet McQuillan?'

'It's Miss actually, yes I'm Janet McQuillan, who is it that I am speaking to?'

'My name is DS Holdsworth from Midshire Police over in Manchester. I understand you called the police with a possible sighting of the two escaped prisoners that we are looking for?'

'Yes, that's correct, they stayed at our bed and breakfast on the night of the 29th December. After they had gone I recognised them from their photographs in the newspaper.'

'What names did they use, Miss McQuillan?'

'Well that's just it, I left them to sign the guest book but I didn't check it until they had left. They signed it as A. Higson and G. Brown but I'm sure they are the prisoners you are looking for.'

'Did they say where they were going to next?'

'Yes, they said they would spend New Year's Eve in Dublin but I'm sure they won't be there.'

'And what makes you think that?'

'Because they were on the wrong platform. I watched them get on the Belfast train.'

CHAPTER 31

Friday 1st January, 2016

'Happy New Year everyone, I trust you all had a good time and you are raring to go without any thick heads this morning,' announced DCI Bentley as he entered the incident room.

'Happy New Year sir,' murmured the muffled response from around the incident room.

'Right, well listen up everyone, at least you have all made it in. I can forgive DS Jones of course as he is still in North Wales. Let me summarise where I think we are. Firstly as you know we have released Father O'Brien without charge, who seems to have a cast iron alibi. We need to do a further interview with Alan Smith from that café as I'm beginning to think he holds the clues as to where our friends Ridgway and Ellis are hiding. As Jean discovered Alan Smith has recently returned from Ireland so we need to follow that line of enquiry up, who did he go and see, did anyone accompany him and more importantly, did he return on his own. Jean, can you see what you can find out, please?'

'I certainly will, sir.'

'That bible found in the cell clearly played a part in this. DC Heath can you please speak to the security guys at the prison and see if they can send us CCTV recordings of the visits that Ridgway had received, i.e. all three visits. I think we need to examine these in detail.'

'Will do, sir.'

'Now we have had positive sightings from Northern Ireland and if my hunch is correct, I think our pair of fugitives are either still there or back here on the mainland,' continued DCI Bentley. 'DS Holdsworth has spoken to the airports and ports security who are on alert and we have asked them to double check any CCTV recordings from 30th December as this was the day they left the B&B and headed towards Belfast. I think we should hear very soon as to whether our pair have moved out of the country. Are there any questions or comments?'

There followed a noticeable silence.

'Good, well let's get back to the job in hand.'

***

DC Bryn Lewis glanced at his watch. It was 3.55pm and the pub was empty, apart from an old gentleman sitting quietly reading a book in the corner.

'I'll have another pint of bitter shandy please, Jeff,' he said, placing his empty glass on the bar.

'Taking it easy Bryn, heavy night last night was it?' asked the barman.

'Yeah, I had a few too many sherbets last night so I'm just pacing myself today.'

Just then the door swung open and in walked Jack Hodgson.

'You must be Bryn Lewis?' said Jack, who was a bit unsure he was even talking to the right person but thought it couldn't be the old man in the corner.

'I am indeed, good to meet you Jack, can I get you a drink?'

'Yes, it's good to meet you, Bryn. I'll just have a pint of bitter shandy, please.'

Bryn signalled to the barman to make it two pints.

'Can we go somewhere quiet Bryn, I know it's empty in here but it's a bit sensitive all this lot.'

'Yes, no problem. I've arranged with Jeff here that we can go into the snug and he'll keep the door closed. How is Pete, by the way? I really enjoyed working with him.'

'Oh, Pete's fine, I haven't seen him for a while and I agree he's a good guy to work with, we've had some good times Pete and myself.'

The two men made their way into a tiny room at the rear of the bar and closed the door behind them.

'So, how can I help you?' enquired Bryn, as he took a seat in a leather armchair next to the fire.

Jack explained to him everything that had gone on, including his surveillance role at the prison and his observations, particularly with regard to Ynys Gwyn. Bryn sat quietly and listened, nodding at various points but leaving Jack to relay the full story.

'So, as you now know Bryn I'm actually on suspension from the force at present but I believe something is going on there, and I don't believe it's involving those escaped prisoners, but I could be wrong of course.'

'Interesting Jack, now what I'm about to tell you can't go anywhere either.'

'Understood.'

'Well, firstly you are right, something is going on there in Dinas Bay and you are also right that it involves smuggling. We know some of the prisoners are most definitely involved, Ridgway and Ellis could be involved as far as I know. We believe the ringleaders also have a network of external contacts who are poised ready and waiting to put their grand scheme into operation. Some of these external contacts are in fact internal if you get my drift, they are in fact prison officers, disturbing I agree, only a couple of them granted. We don't have their names as such but we do have our suspicions. It is only a matter of time before they launch the grand scheme which you will find very disturbing if it were allowed to go ahead. It involves drugs on a very large scale indeed, drugs coming in we believe from Colombia and then being made available through a vast network of dealers throughout major cities and most definitely other prisons. At the moment it is coming in through smaller packages.'

'I guessed it was something along those lines, but how on earth do you know all about this?' replied Jack, who was clearly puzzled at the level of information that Bryn already knew about the situation.

Bryn took a sharp intake of breath. 'Did you ever come across an inmate known as Mick Redfern?'

'Yes a right scruffy bastard, a loud mouth and a nasty piece of work. He was involved in the riot in the chapel just before Christmas. He was on report a couple of times as I remember. Tell me, how do you know Mick Redfern?'

'Because we too have someone in there under cover, it's Mick Redfern. Well that's not his real name of course, he's a Detective Sergeant, Mick is one of us!'

'Bloody hell, who would have thought it, he certainly puts on a good act, he's still in there as far as I know.'

'Yes he is indeed and that's how we want to keep it until all this is sorted. We will then transfer him out of there as quickly as possible but not to another prison of course, he'll need a couple of months off somewhere nice when he eventually comes out. But you have given us some vital information Jack, we didn't know about Ynys Gwyn, we knew it had to be coming in from somewhere but assumed it was coming from a cargo ship somewhere out in the Irish Sea.'

'Well, there is something else which is bothering me a bit.'

'What's that exactly?' replied Bryn, taking a mouthful of shandy.

'Well I'm stopping on this caravan site, Min-y-Coed, not far from the prison and the owner Edward Jones seems to know more than he is letting on.'

Bryn tried desperately not to spurt out a mouthful of beer. 'You're joking, of course I know him, he's reported more suspicious incidents than I've had hot dinners. No you need have no fears there, he's just a nosey old bugger, if we followed up half the incidents he's reported we'd have no resources left.'

'I hoped it might be something like that.'

'I know the place well, Min-y-Coed – the edge of the woodland, nice caravan park. Now look I realise you are under suspension but will you work with us to finally close this lot down?'

'Too bloody right I will.'

'That's excellent Jack, or should I call you John while you are here in North Wales?'

'I think we'd better stick to John for the time being while I'm here in North Wales, you never know who is listening.'

***

'Is that DS Holdsworth?' said the voice on the telephone.

'Yes it is, how can I help you?'

'My name is PC Martin O'Flaherty at Larne Harbour Police. We have been studying the CCTV footage for the 30th December and we believe that the two escaped prisoners that you are looking for passed through the port onto the afternoon Cairnryan ferry at 1.30pm.'

'Were they foot passengers or travelling with a car?'

'They embarked the vessel on foot as far as I'm aware. They were in the foot passenger lounge in the main terminal building.'

'What time would the ferry have docked at Cairnryan?'

'That would be approximately two hours later, I'd say around 3.30pm.'

'Great, that's excellent, thank you Martin. I really appreciate your call, can you please send me screenshots from the recordings as soon as possible.'

'Yes, no problem I plan to send you screen shots from the CCTV later today, I don't have any further information but I suggest you call the police at Stranraer who may be able to give you further information. I'm not familiar with the CCTV coverage at Cairnryan but they should be able to help you.'

'That's great news, thanks again, please pass on my thanks to the other officers involved there.'

DS Holdsworth replaced the receiver and contacted the DCI immediately to tell him the news.

CHAPTER 32

Saturday 2nd January, 2016

DC Heath had obtained the CCTV visitor recordings from the prison and was slowly and carefully browsing through the ones related to the visiting times of Father O'Brien and Alan Smith. He couldn't see anything out of the ordinary at first. He could see in the background some of the prisoners having long lingering kisses with their wife or girlfriend, clearly some sort of personal transfer going on there he thought. And then he noticed something odd, he'd been through each of the visit recordings several times and hadn't noticed it at first. He double checked it to see if his eyes were deceiving him. He picked up the phone and called DS Holdsworth straight away.

'Sarge, I've been going through the visitor recordings as suggested. I can't see anything significant when Alan Smith visited but when Father O'Brien visited the second time he didn't pass through the security scanner, he limped around it.'

'Well what's significant about that? We knew he had a limp, he'd had a motorbike accident several years ago, he has a metal plate in his leg, the DCI had mentioned it in his briefing.'

'Well when he came back the second time, he was limping with his other leg!'

***

DS Holdsworth and DCI Bentley were now on their way to formally arrest Alan Smith at the Jelly Bean café, on suspicion of assisting Ridgeway and Ellis to escape from prison. They had briefly interviewed Bishop O'Reilly, who certainly vouched for Father O'Brien having lunch with him on the 28th November. The attention now had most definitely moved to Alan Smith. The café and the flat upstairs where Alan lived was completely deserted, everywhere was locked up with no sign of anyone at home. A simple sign in the café front window stated *"Closed until further notice"*. DS Holdsworth peered through the side window and it was clear that the place had been abandoned very quickly, there were still half-finished coffee mugs on the tables, chairs all over the place and a pile of dishes waiting to be washed on the counter.

'He must have thrown his customers out looking at this lot, he's done a runner, it is bloody typical,' remarked the DCI. 'He knew we would be on to him sooner or later. Well, we do have his mobile number, when we get back to HQ let's see if he's been stupid enough to use it. I think it's time for us to pack a bag Jim, there is only so much we can do from down here. I'll drop you off home and pick you up, say in an hour's time. We can then call back to HQ for a quick briefing before we head north.'

When they eventually arrived back at the incident room they were in for a further surprise. Stranraer Police had been on the phone to Jean. They too had a CCTV recording of Tim Ridgway, leaving the port terminal building and climbing into a beaten up old Land Rover; what is more they had the vehicle registration as it left the car park.

***

'I'm getting uneasy Charlie, I've just received a text from Alan Smith, he reckons they are onto him and he's gone into hiding,' said Tim, not wishing to share the full content of the text message. 'I mean supposing we have been seen somewhere, there are cameras everywhere and I guess every police force in the land will be on the lookout. For all we know the police could be on their way up here at this very moment.'

'You're right Tim, I think we need to move on fast, well away from here anyway and it's unfair to drag your uncle into all of this. He's been kind enough to pick us up and look after us.'

'I have a plan, Charlie, which I think will throw them off the scent but it's going to mean us splitting up, I'm afraid.'

'Well to be honest, it's probably our best option, Tim, so tell me, what's your plan?'

'Well, it's like this Charlie, I'll get my uncle to drop us off at Carlisle railway station pronto and from there we must go our own separate ways. Remember no communication, in fact I suggest you get yourself a new pay as you go phone and ditch the old one. We'll split the money we have so you should have enough to get by.'

Just then Bill Ridgway appeared and handed out two mugs of tea.

'So how are you lads getting on?'

'Well sorry Bill, I think we have to move out of here quick, I think the police could be onto us, any chance you can run us down to Carlisle railway station?'

'Yes, of course I can Tim, you just give me the word, when do you want to go?'

'Now, please Bill, as soon as possible.'

***

DCI Bentley, as the senior investigating officer, had called an emergency briefing session in the incident room for 1pm for everyone involved on Operation Predator.

'Right this is the situation everyone,' he bellowed. 'DS Holdsworth and I will travel up this afternoon to Dumfries and Galloway to see what the police at Stranraer can give us. Elizabeth my PA has booked the DS and me into a hotel in Dumfries for tonight but who knows where we will end up in the following days. If my guess is right they can't have gone too far in that beaten up Land Rover. However for all we know they could be heading back down here, we might even pass each other on the M6. Now DS Jones will hold the fort down here and liaise with Stranraer Police and us. DC Heath will also remain in the incident room to follow up any CCTV recordings/sightings that come in. We need to get a clearer image of those visitor recordings etc., and of course we need a PNC check on that vehicle at Cairnryan. We will be in touch at all times on our mobiles. Jean, can you analyse Alan Smith's mobile call records, emails etc., anything you can get hold of from the past few days. Finding Alan Smith is secondary of course to us at present as I think we are now getting close to pinning these buggers down. Now if there are no questions or comments DS Holdsworth and I will head up north immediately while the trail is still fresh.'

'Just one thing sir, just a shame you have missed Hogmanay!'

'That had crossed my mind DC Heath, at the rate we are going we might still be investigating this lot on

Burns Night! Anyway perhaps we can celebrate it together when this is finally over.'

'Sounds good to me boss,' announced DS Holdsworth, as he picked up his overnight bag.

***

Jean Price had obtained the mobile phone and landline call records belonging to Alan Smith. She loaded these into the call analysis software and connected the data with the existing transactions database. There were a considerable number of calls from Alan Smith's mobile phone, including several text messages to and from a phone which hadn't previously been encountered. She checked this new number with the service provider and it was a pay as you go phone which had been loaded with a considerable pre-payment. She decided to call Nigel Evans in the CSA (cell site analysis) team. Over the years Cell Site Analysis had become a vital tool for serious and organised crime detection. Reconstructing the location of suspects had proven to be exceptionally powerful with regard to the proximity and patterns of movement in evidence, but today it was needed to ascertain the likely whereabouts of Ridgway and Ellis.

'Hi Nigel, it's Jean Price here, I'm sorry to trouble you on your days off but I wonder if you could please do a history trace on a couple of mobile phones for me, it's rather urgent I'm afraid.'

'Can't it wait until tomorrow?' replied Nigel Evans, who was enjoying his New Year break with his family.

'No, I'm afraid not, I can't explain the operation we are working on as it's confidential and if we leave it too long the opportunity will have been wasted,' she urged.

Nigel Evans sighed, 'Very well, as it's you Jean, I'll be in the office in the next ten minutes.'

Jean set about providing Call Pattern Analysis charts from Alan Smith's phone records. She produced a timeline chart of calls while she waited for Nigel to turn up. It was quite apparent that there had been a flurry of transaction activity on Christmas Eve and she was keen to learn of the locations of the two mobiles at that particular time.

Nigel Evans arrived and started work on the phone records in question. He was not particularly interested in the temporal aspects but more in trying to ascertain the likely locations and paths of the calls from the cell tower dumps. Two hours later he had produced a map which plotted a trail across Wales and Ireland. The trail based on the latest call log ended at present in Dumfries and Galloway, Scotland.

***

'John, it's Bryn Lewis, are you available later on this evening?'

'Yes, why, have there been any developments?'

'Well yes and no, we have had it on good authority from our man on the inside that a smuggling run is being discussed and it could be happening tonight. It might not be of course, as we've had these false alarms before, but we have to follow it up. If we pick you up, say at 7pm, do you think you can remember where you saw that couple loading boxes into that 4x4?'

'Yes, no problem, I'll be at the caravan at that address I gave you earlier.'

'Great, I'll see you later.'

***

DCI Bentley and DS Holdsworth had belted up the M6 and had now arrived at Stranraer Police station. The DS had driven all the way in what proved to be a relatively easy journey up the M6 motorway. In fact the only disturbance was the DCI's snoring as they headed north. On the journey up they had been kept informed of the developments including the analysis of call records from Alan Smith's phone. They parked up in front of the modern two storey building and checked in with the duty officer on the front desk. Stranraer Police had clearly been told of their imminent arrival and were ready to welcome them. The desk sergeant led them through to a long corridor leading to a number of ground floor offices. Immediately they were welcomed into the conference room by Chief Inspector Leach, a tall thick-set man in his early fifties, who had clearly been round the block a few times.

'So, good evening gentlemen and welcome to Stranraer,' said the Chief Inspector. 'Now, I'm sure you've had quite a long journey and would appreciate some tea or coffee before we start,' signalling over to the desk sergeant who was just about to return to the front desk.

'Yes, that would be lovely, I'm quite parched,' replied DCI Bentley as he and DS Holdsworth took a seat opposite him.

The two Midshire officers then briefed the Chief Inspector on the prison escape, the background of the prisoners and the belief they were in the county.

Ten minutes later the door swung open and the desk sergeant arrived with a welcoming tray of tea, coffee and biscuits.

'Well we've also got some video footage to show you that I'm sure you will be interested in,' said the Chief Inspector, switching on the large flat screen in the corner. 'You will see here the moment Ridgway leaves the terminal building and walks across the car park to the waiting vehicle, clearly pre-arranged of course. Now there is a gap of say no more than ten minutes but we'll fast forward it and you will see Ellis now emerging, clearly not sure of what he could expect when he comes out of the building, in fact he looks lost. Then Ellis notices a flash of headlights at the far end of the car park and makes his way over to the Land Rover. The vehicle is registered to a Mr William Ridgway who has an address in the Forest of Galloway, about an hour away from here. Two of my officers are already en route to that address as we speak. They have been instructed not to do anything on arrival but to wait until instructed.'

'That's excellent,' remarked DCI Bentley,' I suggest we follow them up as soon as possible and make the arrest. I don't believe they are dangerous but you can never be sure.'

'Well, we'll have this drink and be on our way,' said the Chief Inspector, taking one of the cups.

'Just one question sir,' asked DS Holdsworth, 'does this William Ridgway who is presumably related to Tim have any previous convictions that we should be aware of?'

'Yes, I'm afraid to say he does, he has been previously arrested for possession of an illegal firearm about a year ago!'

'Right, I think the sooner we visit Mr Ridgway the better, come on drink up Jim, time is of the essence,' remarked the DCI, who was keen to get back on the road.

Jim drank the hot tea as quickly as he could and they started to make their way out of the police station. They were just at the front door when the Chief Inspector stopped to receive a phone call. The three officers stood there, motionless.

'That was PC Woodman, who is one of the two officers we despatched to watch Ridgway's place. You are not going to believe this but he said just as they arrived at the farmhouse a 4x4 matching William Ridgway's vehicle description was driving off in the opposite direction towards Dumfries. They weren't sure at first whether it was actually Ridgway's vehicle and they couldn't see who or how many people were in the vehicle but the farmhouse is now empty. Our officers are now in pursuit but it's my guess they will have lost them down the many side roads in the area. I'll put an alert out to all officers to watch for the vehicle. My guess is that they are heading to a mainline train station which could either be Dumfries or Carlisle. If we get a move on we should be able to catch them, en route.' Just as they piled into the car DS Holdsworth also took a call on his mobile.

'Right we are on to it straight away, keep texting me the location Nigel, as it changes,' shouted the DS, 'we are on our way.'

'It's the tower dump guys, the last signal from the phone is coming from a village outside Dumfries, step on the gas quick!'

***

DC Clive Heath was still busy trying to manually identify who it was that had visited Ridgway in prison. Clearly Father O'Brien had visited the first time but he had a cast iron alibi at the time of the second visit. DC Heath then hit on the idea of running an automated facial recognition scan across the recordings. He opened up two windows on the computer and in the right window loaded in the paused video frame of Father O'Brien's second visit on the 28th November.

In the left hand window he loaded up the other video recordings he had received from the prison. Using the mouse he clicked on the frozen image of Father O'Brien and selected the match option from the facial recognition software. Immediately as the video ran the software started picking out each of the faces in the left hand window that could be seen, even those of prison officers. Five minutes later a positive array of photographs in sorted order appeared. There was absolutely no doubt about it, the facial image of Father O'Brien had been matched to Alan Smith.

***

Bryn Lewis arrived exactly on the hour at the caravan park to pick up John Hughes and soon they were heading off down a country lane towards the village of Trefor. They were followed by two other police officers as backup in a further unmarked police car.

'What support can we expect Bryn?' asked John Hughes, as they drove in the darkness towards the shoreline.

'Well in addition to the two officers who are following behind us, I've arranged for the NCA Marine police patrol boat to be moored outside the harbour at Trefor. I've also arranged for the coastguard to be on watch should we need them. They will be out of sight of course but I don't want to lose these buggers,' he responded.

'It's just coming up on the right hand side, down that track,' said John Hughes, 'just here. I suggest both cars park up further down the main road towards the village and the two of us go off on foot, we can liaise with the other two officers to come and block the track if our suspicions are correct.'

Bryn Lewis briefed the two officers accordingly and he set off with John Hughes down the dirt track in the direction of the clifftop. They found a suitable vantage point amongst the rocks part way down to the beach and waited there patiently.

'Did you see that?' whispered John Hughes, 'a light out at sea, there, there it is again.'

Sure enough out on the near horizon a light flashed just once and moments later they heard a vehicle pulling up on the clifftop just above them. They crouched down and watched while a man and a woman edged their way steadily down the gravel path to the beach below. They could now see the light of a small fishing boat getting nearer and nearer. The next thing the two people had waded straight into the cold water to meet the boat as it came in as close as it could. Two large boxes were passed to them from the fishing boat and were subsequently carried onto the beach.

Bryn Jones radioed to the two officers to block the farm track gateway and to alert his counterpart in the Marine section to intercept the fishing boat as it headed back out.

'Shall we take them now?' whispered John Hughes, as the two figures inched their way up the path to the vehicle.

'No, we'll stop them at the gateway to the track, there is no other way out of here. They won't get far.'

They watched as the 4x4 made its way slowly down the rough farm track and saw the brake lights come on at the entrance. By the time Bryn and John had arrived on foot at the gateway the driver was now out of his vehicle arguing with one of the police officers. He was refusing to let the officer examine the boxes in the back of the vehicle and demanding that the police officer allow him through.

'Can you please open the back of the vehicle, sir?' said Bryn Lewis, who now took over the situation.

'Who the bloody hell are you? No, you have no right to stop me, this is private land,' came the reply.

John Hughes thought he recognised the voice but it was dark with no street lighting at the entrance to the track. All this time the woman in the passenger seat sat quietly, not uttering a word.

'We have every right sir, now are you going to co-operate or perhaps you would like to continue this conversation back at the police station.'

The man, who could see no way out of the situation, opened up the rear of the vehicle. DC Lewis opened up one of the cardboard boxes and there under torchlight was a huge haul of cocaine, all carefully packed in one kilo packages. The woman by now had got out of the vehicle and was thinking of making a run for it but realised quickly it was futile.

'You are both under arrest on suspicion of smuggling drugs into the country. You do not have to say anything. But it may harm your defence if you do not mention when questioned something which you later rely on in court. Anything you do say may be given in evidence.'

The two of them and the boxes were now both bundled into the back of the waiting police car and taken off to Caernarvon police station.

***

Tim Ridgway and Charlie Ellis were now being driven at great speed through tiny villages down narrow country lanes and the occasional farm tracks. It was now going dark and they were just passing through a small village in the middle of nowhere.

'Bill, can you stop here for just a minute?'

'Why, do you feel ill, Tim? I'm afraid the route is a bit twisting and winding but I thought I'd use the back roads to avoid any road block checks just in case the police are on to you.'

'No, I just need to pop into this phone box for a second.'

Bill Ridgway pulled up in a nearby layby on the right hand side. Tim walked back and entered the phone box. Minutes later he was back in the vehicle.

'What on earth is that all that about?' asked Charlie.

'I just needed to get rid of that mobile phone, I've left it on and hidden it in there, at least it may just give us extra time as a diversion to get away. How much further now, Bill?'

'Well I'm taking this route across country to avoid the route that the police are likely to use to come to the farmhouse,' said Bill Ridgway, 'it's a bit further but we should join the A75 main road at Dumfries, from there it should only take us about 50 minutes to the train station.'

'Thanks Bill, we really do appreciate this but what will you do after you have dropped us off?' said Tim.

'I'll go back and face the consequences. I'll plead ignorance and just say that I didn't even know you were on the run. It won't be long now lads, hold on tight.'

Eventually, after what seemed like a lifetime, they arrived in a side street just around the corner from

Carlisle railway station and all three got out and said their farewells.

'I think this where the three of us all go our own separate ways now. Thanks ever so much Bill, for helping us out,' said Tim, shaking his hand and anxiously looking round to make sure no one had spotted them.

'Well you look after yourselves, boys, I'll try and stall the police as much as I can. It's been good to see you again Tim, hope it all works out for you both,' replied Bill Ridgway as he got back into the vehicle and drove off at high speed.

'Well, I'm heading north, up to Glasgow, I'll find somewhere to doss down,' said Charlie, not knowing where exactly he would end up.

'I'm going south Charlie, I'll be in touch when it's safe but you look after yourself, I will contact you via this dropbox account that I have set up for both of us,' said Tim, as he handed Charlie a slip of paper.

'Thanks Tim, you have a safe journey,' replied Charlie as he pocketed the note.

'We need to separate from here so you go into the station first,' said Tim, as they shook hands for one last time.

Charlie made his way down the street and entered the station building. He made his way through into the ticket hall, booked his ticket and headed over to platform 3.

Tim waited for a few minutes, bought his ticket and headed off to platform 1.

***

The two police cars were now hurtling across the A75 at great speed with blues and twos blaring as they took the turning off towards the village of Thornhill.

'We have had a cell phone signal from here not long ago,' shouted DS Holdsworth, 'it's possible they have gone to ground again around here somewhere but it's worth a shot.'

Just as they sped into the village they received a radio call from Dumfries police saying that Bill Ridgway's Land Rover had now been spotted the other side of Dumfries. It was clear they were now on a wild goose chase, there was the solitary phone box. Nevertheless DS Holdsworth quickly dashed into the phone box and there was the mobile phone for all to see.

'Come on, we've wasted enough time here,' he said grabbing the phone, 'it's my guess they are on the way to the train station.'

An hour later they approached Carlisle railway station and could see a Landrover fitting the description of Bill Ridgway's vehicle speeding off in the opposite direction.

'That was Bill Ridgway's vehicle, I'm sure,' said Chief Inspector Leach as they came to a halt, 'let's just hope the trains are delayed and we can catch the buggers on the platform.'

The police officers dashed into the station and arrived at platform 1. There was not a soul to be seen apart from a railway worker loading a large parcel onto a trolley.

'You've missed the last train south, gentlemen, next one is at 5.30am,' said the porter as he pushed the trolley into the office.

'Bloody typical,' boomed DCI Bentley, 'missed them by seconds. I'm assuming they are both travelling south, I'll get onto the transport police.'

***

Tim didn't have to wait long for the First Transpine Express to Manchester. He took a seat in the First Class carriage, it was quiet apart from an old couple who were travelling back home after their Christmas break. As the train sped through the Lake District he decided to send a quick text.

'Should arrive at Airport tonight will text you later with the ETA, meet you as arranged outside on the departure ramp at T2.'

He didn't have to wait long before the response came back.

'Everything in hand, will see you there.'

CHAPTER 33

Sunday 3rd January, 2016

Tim Ridgway had arrived at Manchester Airport just after midnight. The train had been delayed for some unknown reason outside Preston. For a moment Tim had panicked, thinking any moment now the Transport Police would be coming through the carriage to arrest him. He stepped off the train at the airport and took the Skylink walkway to Terminal 2. Sure enough waiting there for him with a suitcase as planned was Alan Smith.

'Sorry I'm late Alan, did you manage to get me the paperwork I needed?'

'No problem Tim, yes, it's all here just as you requested, passport, visa, tickets and credit cards,' said Alan, handing over the documents and the suitcase. 'I think you'll find everything you need here including your pass for the business lounge. I've booked you in as arranged under the name you gave me at the airport hotel so I suggest you have a few hours' sleep before the check-in desk opens at 6am. Have a great trip and keep in touch when you can.'

'Thanks Alan, I owe you one.'

Alan then flagged down a taxi and headed off into the night.

Tim made his way across to the Airport Hotel up the escalator to the reception desk.

'Good evening or rather, good morning, sir, and how may I help you?' said the receptionist politely.

'I'm booked in for one night, leaving early in the morning.'

'And what name is it under sir?'

'The name is Paul Arrowsmith.'

***

John Hughes and DC Bryn Lewis had followed the police car and the 4x4 to Caernarvon police station where the two people were now being held in custody for questioning. The marine police section had also arrested two men outside the harbour at Trefor and these were currently being escorted to Caernarvon for interviewing.

John Hughes, as he was under suspension, decided to wait in the CID office and leave Bryn Lewis to firstly question the driver of the Land Rover. Bryn had been in the interview room for over thirty minutes and eventually emerged frustrated.

'He's telling us nothing,' said DC Lewis as he entered the CID office, 'not even his name, it's like getting blood out of stone. Everything I put to him comes out as no comment, perhaps you could come in and we'll both have a go, he might take more notice of you, he's still under caution.'

'Well, I am officially under suspension, but yes if it helps I'll come in with you,' replied John Hughes.

They made their way down the corridor into the room marked interview room number one. John Hughes followed DC Bryn Lewis into the room where a police constable and a duty solicitor were accompanying the offender. As John entered the room he was shocked by what he saw. He knew he had recognised that voice from somewhere.

'Hello Greg, fancy meeting you here, I thought I recognised that voice.'

'Interview continued at 12.45am,' said DC Lewis switching back on the voice recorder, 'joining me in the room is DC Hodgson from Midshire Police.'

Jack realised at this point that his cover was blown but he didn't care; he had no intention of going back into the prison or using the name John Hughes again.

'John!' stammered Greg Henderson, 'what are you doing here and what's all this DC Hodgson business, don't tell me you are in on this?'

'Yes, I'm very much in on this, Greg, but not in the same capacity as you are I am pleased to say.'

Greg Henderson was stunned and still hadn't taken it in that John Hughes had in fact been working under cover.

'DC Lewis, can I introduce you to relief prison officer Greg Henderson from HMP Dinas Bay.'

'Well, fancy that, so that's where the drugs were destined for!' exclaimed DC Lewis, drawing up a chair.

Greg Henderson decided that he now had no option but to come clean and he poured out the whole story to the three police officers in the room. He told the officers that he had hit on the idea when a fisherman from Anglesey approached him in the local pub, telling him that he could source drugs big style. His accomplices encouraged him to bring in drugs and the plan was to distribute them across the entire prison system in the region. It had started with just the odd package and had grown out of all proportion from there. He didn't have details on where the drugs were actually coming from and believed they were being dropped off after a rendezvous with a Colombian container ship. They were stored in bulk somewhere off shore. As far as distribution was concerned he was in the ideal position as he worked across multiple prisons. For this he was being paid handsomely.

'So who is your accomplice, your lady friend in the next room?' asked DC Lewis.

'You'll have to ask her won't you, but it's possible John here might recognise her,' replied Henderson, who was frantically biting his nails.

'We will do exactly that Mr Henderson, we will be back in a minute. For the purpose of the tape recording this interview is suspended at 12.55 a.m.'

Jack Hodgson and Bryn Lewis made their way down the corridor into interview room two and that's when Jack got the second shock of the night. There, sitting sobbing into her handkerchief, was Helen Morris.

***

DCI Bentley and DS Holdsworth were exhausted, they had managed to get at least a few hours' sleep at the hotel in Dumfries after the chase for Ridgway and Ellis went cold. The two officers were having breakfast in the hotel when the DCI received a phone call from British Transport Police in Glasgow Central station saying that after a tip off they had arrested Charlie Ellis just as he was about to board a train to Inverness.

'Keep him bloody there, we are on our way,' shouted the DCI down the phone to the police officer. DCI Bentley was furious that Ridgway and Ellis had left the Dumfries area without even being spotted. 'At least we've got one of them but where the hell is Ridgway? I mean he can't have disappeared, can he?'

'Well it's my guess he's gone in the opposite direction, sir,' replied DS Holdsworth, who was now tucking into his cooked breakfast, 'but we've had no reported sightings, he's probably well away by now. Maybe Ellis will give us a few clues.'

'Ridgway's bloody uncle knows more than he's telling us as well, he'll be charged later today, thank God. Come on, finish your breakfast, we are on our way to Glasgow, any idea how long it will take us Jim?'

'I reckon we should be at Glasgow Central station in about ninety minutes time, all being well and providing that toast I ordered turns up, sir.'

***

Bryn Lewis and Jack Hodgson had decided there was just one more vital piece of the jigsaw outstanding and that was the storage of drugs which either had to have come from a ship waiting out in the bay or stored long term on the island of Ynys Gwyn. Bryn organised for the 15m police patrol boat and a naval vessel from Holyhead to take them out to the island as soon as it was first light. Jack was not looking forward to the journey, he'd been violently ill the last time he went out there. And so at 7am, accompanied by four other police officers, they boarded the police vessel and headed off at high speed to the island. The weather was kinder for this journey and the boat considerably faster than the little fishing boat. Within thirty minutes they were moored up alongside the old stone jetty at Ynys Gwyn. They stepped onto the jetty this time armed with suitable tools and made their way up the carved out stone steps, through the wooded area to the old monastery at the summit. Jack took them around the side to the small oak doorway. Jack noticed that since his last visit someone had attempted to hide the entrance by dragging tree branches in front of it. The officers removed these and set about prising open the huge lock on the door. Eventually after several attempts it gave way and they pushed open the door. The place was as expected in darkness and DC Lewis shone a torch light into the cobweb-festooned cellar. There piled floor to ceiling were boxes and boxes sealed with duct tape. They opened up one of the boxes and discovered about 500 bags of cocaine. There was quite simply tons of the stuff. The officers formed a chain to carry the boxes down to the waiting boats and once the cellar was cleared they set off back to Caernarvon. In total they estimated they had moved in excess of three tons of drugs with a street value of over £500 million.

'So, where are you for now Jack, will you have time for a celebratory drink with us later?' asked Bryn Lewis as they arrived back at the caravan.

'No thanks Bryn, I'm exhausted, I'm going for a sleep now for a few hours before heading back home to the wife and family, but it's been good working with you and please keep in touch. I couldn't have done this without your help.'

'Likewise Jack, we owe you a big one. I'm sure we'll be in touch,' said DC Lewis, shaking hands before he drove off.

Jack Hodgson opened up the caravan and was about to step inside when almost like magic Edward Jones appeared from around the side of the van.

'Been out all night fishing have we, Mr Hughes?'

'Something like that Mr Jones, something like that.'

***

News of the huge drugs haul soon got back to DCI Bentley and DS Holdsworth, who were now on their way back from Glasgow. They had interviewed Charlie Ellis but he had told them nothing that they hadn't already worked out. All Charlie knew was that Tim Ridgway had gone south, that was all he could tell them, that was all he knew himself. The prisoner escort service had arrived to take Ellis on the long journey back to the North Wales prison. The DCI and DS were now also heading down the M6 back to Midshire Police HQ.

'Well I'm bloody embarrassed to be honest, Jim, I should have taken notice of Jack, he was closer to it than we were. I've learnt a valuable lesson here and I know one thing; I'd like him back in CID as soon as possible and I'll assure him his undercover days are well and truly over. I'm recommending he puts in for his sergeant's examination again, he certainly has the right

311

qualities,' said the DCI. 'I shall give him a personal call when we get back home.'

'He will appreciate that I'm sure sir, he's done a fine job guv, and you certainly can't question his commitment, I mean going back there when he was on suspension, not every copper would do that.'

***

Jack Hodgson was back where he wanted to be, back with his family and in the comfort of his own home. He was starting to get his own life back again, he knew he had a lot of making up to do with his family. DCI Bentley had called him to thank him for all his efforts and to welcome him back into the CID fold. Sue hadn't realised he had even been suspended but she suspected something was not quite as it should be. In the meantime school half-term was approaching next month and Sue was planning a holiday for them all to get away again.

'Do you know where I fancy going this time, Jack?' said Sue, who was leafing through various brochures, newspapers and magazines.

'No, where is that Sue?'

'Well do you remember those lovely family holidays we had in North Wales, I fancy going back there. What do you think?'

'No, maybe next year Sue, maybe next year, I fancy flying off somewhere, a bit of sun abroad would be good.'

***

The Singapore Airlines Boeing 777 plane SQ327 at Manchester Airport pushed back from Terminal 2 gate 210 at 9.20am and taxied to runway 23L. The flight took off exactly on schedule at 09.45 for the fifteen hour journey, heading first for Munich and then onwards to Singapore. Paul Arrowsmith settled back in seat 16A in business class, sipping a glass of champagne. For now the heat was well and truly off but Paul had other things on his mind.

EPILOGUE

Monday 4th January, 2016

A criminal who escaped from a Category 'C' prison has been arrested yesterday in Glasgow and returned to the prison in North Wales. Charlie Ellis had been on the run since fleeing from HMP Dinas Bay, North Wales on December 24th 2015.

A statement from Midshire Police issued this afternoon stated that "Charles Ellis from the Manchester area, was arrested yesterday morning at Glasgow Central railway station as he tried to board a train to Inverness and has now been taken into custody."

Ellis, who was serving a sentence for fraud and identity theft, had been missing since around 9pm on Christmas Eve.

A second man, Timothy John Ridgway, who escaped with Ellis is still on the run but is now believed to be out of the country.

Thursday 14th July, 2016

Two prison officers today were convicted at Mold Crown Court of the intent to supply drugs across a number of prisons in the North West. Relief Prison Officer Greg Henderson and Prison Officer Helen Morris were each sentenced to serve ten years' imprisonment.

Two men from the Anglesey area, John Edward Ellis and Bernard Ross, were also convicted of drug smuggling and each sentenced to five years' imprisonment.

Two brothers aged 14 and 12 have admitted flying a drone into the exercise yard in HMP Dinas Bay. The brothers, who cannot be named for legal reasons, pleaded guilty to the offence and will be sentenced later this month.

A 65-year-old man from Dumfries and Galloway received a twelve month suspended prison sentence today for helping two escaped prisoners. William Ridgway assisted his nephew Timothy Ridgway and Charlie Ellis in their escape from HMP Dinas Bay.

***

Alan Smith, a 45-year-old Manchester businessman was today sentenced to five years in prison for helping two inmates escape from HMP Dinas Bay. The two inmates, Timothy John Ridgway and Charlie Ellis, escaped on Christmas Eve 2015. Smith provided the tools used in their break-out which included the supply of hacksaw blades. Ellis has since been recaptured but Ridgway remains on the run.